FOREST OF THE SASQUATCH 3

THE UPRISING

LUKA T. JACOBS

*"Vengeance is in my heart, death in my hand,
blood, and revenge are hammering in my head."*

William Shakespeare, *Titus Andronicus*

FROM THE AUTHOR

Hey there, fearless reader!

Thank you for picking up *Forest of the Sasquatch 3: The Uprising*. This finale will hit hardest if you have already braved the shadowed timber of Books 1 and 2. If you have not taken that trek yet, consider this a friendly nudge to start at the beginning so every roar, tree knock and hard-won victory lands the way it should.

I am an indie author fueled by back-and-forth midnight chats with my dog, Finnigan, cryptid documentaries and your support. Reviews, messages and reader enthusiasm keep these pages turning. Want to swap theories or get a peek at future projects? Join me on **Facebook** or sign up for my **newsletter** and let us keep the conversation alive.

Happy reading!

Luka T. Jacobs

CONTENTS

PROLOGUE

The bang snapped James Jackson awake.

What sounded like an open-handed blow cracked against the cedar siding below his bedroom window, hard enough to rattle the water glass on the nightstand.

Could have been a loose branch, he told himself, though the night was calm. He sat up in bed, rubbed his eyes, and stayed still, listening hard for footsteps or any other sound. Maybe it was someone who had drifted up from the highway half a mile south. He listened another minute, heartbeat still fast, then swung his legs over the edge and padded across the hall to the spare room. Moonlight pooled on the floorboards. He parted the curtain an inch. The porch light cast a pale square on the grass. Nothing moved. No branches swayed.

James watched until his calves cramped, then went back to bed. Sleep never returned. At dawn he brewed coffee, then circled the house. On the east wall three palm-shaped dents bowed the siding, each higher than he could reach. He studied the marks and walked the grass. No footprints, no trash, no tire ruts.

Two quiet nights followed, and he had almost put the incident out of his mind.

On the third, three blows struck the kitchen wall minutes past midnight, heavier than the first. Pots rattled on their hooks. Again, the silence that followed felt unnatural. James got up, moved quietly through the house, and checked each window he passed. He stepped carefully into the kitchen and stood still, straining to hear anything beyond the ticking of the clock and the thud of his own pulse. Nothing moved.

Morning showed a single footprint in damp soil beneath the kitchen window. Five toes, narrow heel, twenty inches long. Something about its depth and the spread of the toes tightened a knot inside him. The woods beyond suddenly looked darker, as if the pines themselves leaned closer.

He photographed the print and pinned the picture above his workbench.

A week of uneasy calm followed. During daylight he mounted two trail cameras on posts facing the treeline.

Nights stayed hot. Summer heat baked the forest and sweat dampened his sheets long before dawn. No fresh strikes came.

Seven nights later, footsteps thundered across the roof. Six heavy strides pounded shingles, then a single leap into the driveway gravel. James jolted upright, heart racing. For a moment he thought it might've been raccoons or even a black bear, but the weight of it didn't sit right. Too heavy. Too controlled.

By the time he reached the porch with the flashlight, the yard lay empty. In the morning he found claw grooves slashed through the asphalt shingles. He traced each gouge with a fingertip, feeling the depth, and taped another Polaroid beside the first.

The cries came next. Raw, high screams drifted from behind the shed, too shrill for a cougar and too human for any fox or coyote. They rose in twos and threes, sounding like something dying slowly in the dark. Some of them lasted nearly thirty seconds. James stood on the porch, both hands clenched around the stock. Whatever was making that sound, he thought, had lungs like a bull moose and no intention of hiding. It wasn't moving. It was staying in the tree line. He counted each call until the night fell silent again.

The next day, he replaced the porch bulbs with new

motion lights and added two more cameras. Footage showed only swaying branches, yet batteries drained faster than expected. At dusk he sometimes heard a perfect barred-owl hoot when he stepped outside or the moment he rolled his truck into the drive. Four notes, pause, four notes. The call never moved closer, always at the boundary as if marking his arrival. Each time, the hoots sounded just a little off. Not enough to notice at first, but there was something mechanical in them, something not quite right at the end of each call.

He thought of the wooden crate stored in the basement, the one he had inherited when his old Vietnam buddy passed away two winters earlier. Inside sat six claymore mines, still packed in grease, along with a coil of firing wire and a battered clacker switch. He had promised himself the crate would stay sealed unless things ever turned truly bad. Standing on the porch with owl calls echoing through the timber, he wondered if it was time to pry the lid open.

The property settled into an eerie lull. Trail cams stayed blank. No prints marked the bare soil near the shed. Deer avoided the garden entirely. The hush felt like a breath held too long.

One afternoon, James decided to walk into the timber and have a look. He took his rifle, slinging it over one shoulder, and followed an old game trail that ran along the edge of the property. After an hour of trudging beneath the thick canopy, he realized he hadn't seen so much as a rabbit. No birds. No insects. The woods felt off. Void of all life. Every branch seemed too still, too quiet, as if the forest itself were listening.

As he turned to head back, he heard it, footfalls, heavy and steady, off to his right. The brush was thick in that direction, a tangle of pine and undergrowth, and the canopy overhead blocked what little sun remained. James stopped walking. The steps stopped too.

He tested it. Three slow paces forward. Then silence. Another two, and the crunching resumed. Matched him step for step.

He brought the rifle up and looked through the scope, sweeping the area beyond the trees. Nothing moved, but every hair on his neck stood on end. Then he felt it. The growl. It vibrated through the ground, through his boots, through his ribs. Deep. Primal. Animalistic.

James backed away slowly, rifle still raised. He didn't run. Not yet. But he walked faster with every step, glancing behind him every few paces. When the trees broke and his backyard came into view, he ran.

Inside the house, he shut the back door, locked it, and

moved straight to the window. Peering through the glass, he caught a glimpse of something crouched near a pine at the edge of the yard. A shape. No features. Just a dark, hunched mass in the shadows.

He stared at it for five minutes, unmoving. It didn't flinch. Didn't step forward. Eventually, James backed away and went to sit down, his heart still hammering.

Two nights later, midnight rain drummed on the roof. Between gusts, James heard a different patter, small stones striking siding and window glass. First a light scatter, then a fistful at once, flung with force from unseen hands. The impacts moved from the north wall to the west, tapping at one corner then another, as if testing every side of the house.

Over the hiss of rain he heard running on the roof again, two separate sets of footsteps crossing the length of the shingles. Something heavy dropped into the yard. Another blow slammed the plywood over the kitchen window.

James stepped into the mudroom, flicked the safety off his rifle, and waited. Lightning flashed, revealing a silhouette at the corner of the shed. Shoulders broader than the fridge, head brushing the eave. He brought up the rifle but the creature vanished around the corner in an instant.

The next couple of nights stayed still and the cameras

showed nothing.

The night before he saw the creature for the last time, he woke to a hard knock on his bedroom window. He sat up, heart hammering, and shone his flashlight at the glass. No shape moved outside, only a patch of white moisture where a snout or nose had breathed against the pane. By the time he got up, the mist was gone. He sat on the edge of the bed, shotgun across his lap, until dawn.

The next evening he prepared differently. He propped his bedroom window open two inches and climbed into bed fully dressed, shotgun cradled against his chest. It was loaded with double-aught buckshot. He wasn't going to take chances. He watched the gap where dark met frame until exhaustion claimed him in short, shallow dozes.

Around three in the morning a foul stench drifted through the opening, wet dog and rotting garbage baking in the sun. His eyes snapped open. No light but a thin glow from the moon. He could see the window clearly but the dark frame hid him. He stared at the massive hand sliding into view, thick with two inch long patchy black and brown matted hair and gray skin dotted with scars. The creature paused, then pushed the window open a little farther. Its wrist slid through the opening, fingers sweeping the air as if searching. James's grip tightened on the stock.

His gaze locked on the beast's long, dirty nails. A low, wet sniff sounded at the pane. In the next instant the arm recoiled and James squeezed the trigger. The blast ripped through the room. Splinters flew from the sill.

A monstrous scream echoed into the night as heavy footfalls thundered away across the yard. James sat frozen, shoulders tense, shotgun still raised. His ears rang from the shot, but beneath that, he could hear his pulse thudding in his neck. He stared at the window, waiting for the arm to return, for another shape to rise out of the dark.

Nothing came.

Within minutes the forest slipped back into its familiar rhythms. Crickets resumed their soft chirps and even the wind took a breath.

James stayed upright the rest of the night, shotgun in hand, listening until first light. Morning revealed dark smears on the grass below the window and splintered wood at the sill. He knelt in the yard and smelled iron. He knew he had hit it.

Later, he sat on the porch with a coffee going cold in his hand. This had been his home for twenty years. After the divorce and early retirement, all he'd wanted was space. Peace. To be left the hell alone.

But now the woods had changed.

He finished the coffee, stood, and headed down to the basement. Dust coated the crate. He pried the lid open, removed one claymore, and placed it on the workbench. He did not wire it yet, but seeing it there eased something inside him.

They would be back.

He intended to be ready.

CHAPTER 1

THE DAY AFTER THE OLD ONE FELL

The blood no longer hung in the air, though its scent still lingered in the dirt where the Elder had fallen. The forest had turned quiet. The trees had gone into mourning.

Aluk stood motionless on the ridge above the Sanctuary cave, shoulders gathering snow. Below, the troop assembled: some females were inside the cave tending to the wounded, while others stood at the entrance with yearlings pressed to their sides. Fifteen warriors ringed the clearing, hair still streaked with the night's battle. None spoke. The Elder deserved more than silence, yet Aluk did not descend. He watched from afar. He would not share in the rite.

Two senior females washed the Elder with melted snow, combing knots from his silver hair with spruce needles, then tucking crow feathers behind one ear. Balsam resin sealed the deepest wounds so carrion scent would not reach the treeline. Laid upon a cedar plank bier, the Elder looked merely asleep, hands folded, chest still as stone.

Three juveniles set river stones in a perfect ring around the bier, each one nudged tight against the next until no gap remained. Elders said such stones carried heartbeats back into the soil.

Four matriarchs approached with birch-bark bundles tied in sinew. Inside lay obsidian shards lifted from the ancient flow ridges near the big water. The bundles were placed at the Elder's folded hands so the glassy rock could guide him in the dark.

Using fresh pine boughs, the matriarchs brushed sticky needles across his chest. Pitch-soaked hair and skin, forming a green mantle that trapped the scent of living trees.

When preparations ended, two warriors gripped the bier's cedar handles. They bore the Elder through the cave entrance into a stone chamber lit only by faint lichen glow. At the heart of that chamber yawned a natural shaft dropping beyond sight, believed to be the place their kind had first stepped out of the earth.

The warriors eased the bier over the edge. River stones

slid first, clacking in darkness. Obsidian bundles followed, catching the last glimmer of light as they fell. Finally the Elder's body slipped into the void, feathers fluttering once before the darkness swallowed them. A distant boom rose from the depths, then silence.

The troop sealed the shaft. Heavy limestone slabs, pried earlier from the chamber wall, were levered into place. Snow was packed into seams and smeared with resin until the closure appeared part of the cave itself. Only then did the warriors back away, foreheads touching the cold rock once in farewell.

Aluk stood above the clearing, apart from the others. They had gathered near the cave where the Elder once stood, tall and unmoving, the one they looked to when the seasons changed or when the ground whispered of danger. Now there was only stillness, and unease.

It had begun snowing that morning, a silent drift of white descending without urgency. The first deep snow of the season.

Aluk did not brush the snow from his hair or shake the cold from his arms. He stood motionless, as if carved from the stone beneath his feet.

Fifteen males stood nearer the front, the last of those

strong enough to fight. One had a torn ear, another a wrist bound in strips of bark, but the blood from any wounds had long since crusted.

Aluk raised one arm, fingers curled, then spread wide.

A sound followed, not loud but full in the chest, a call to come forward.

They climbed the slope toward him, their steps steady, placing feet with care as they crossed the roots and thin crust of snow. Their movements were fluid, aided by a mid-foot hinge that let them grip and balance with ease, unlike any human. They formed a loose half-circle, waiting without sound.

Aluk cast the first image into their minds.

The cave, not as it was now, but how it had been, when the Elder stood tall at its entrance, his hands folded, his breath slow, his silence full of meaning.

He cast the second image, clear and sharp. The broken ones. The dead lying still on the cold earth, limbs twisted, faces quiet. The young who would never grow tall. The ones who had not even been named.

Then came the thunder sticks. Flashes that split the trees. Sound that crushed the air and left nothing behind but torn bodies and scorched ground.

Some of the fifteen grunted softly. Others lowered their eyes. One crouched, claws sinking into the frozen soil.

Aluk cast the final image. The places of the hairless ones. Their cold paths, their square dens, the growling metal beasts that tore through the forest without care. He showed the scent of them, how it clung to the trees long after they were gone.

He struck his chest once, then grunted and chattered low in his throat. Raising two fingers, he pointed west.

Go. Bring the others. Not from this clan, but from the far places. The quiet branches. The ones who had kept to themselves.

They split into three groups of five.

One turned toward the icy cliffs of Gooseberry. One to the thicker shadows of Tettegouche. The last toward the deep, wet ground of Finland.

Aluk did not watch them vanish. He crouched beside a stone and placed both hands on his knees, his eyes open and fixed on the distant edge of the woods. The snow moved across his shoulders. He stayed there, watching.

CHAPTER 2

The group that moved toward Gooseberry climbed in silence. The path was not theirs, but they knew it. Old trails, shaped by time and use, led through narrow valleys where trees thinned and leaned. Ahead, bent birch limbs crossed in an arch, the first signal that Gooseberry ground lay near. Two more arches followed, each angle sharper than the last, branches woven so no passing creature could miss the warning or lose direction. When the bark changed scent and the soil grew unfamiliar, they stopped.

The largest among them stepped forward. He pressed his fists to his chest once, again, then a third time. He turned to a tall tree and dragged his knuckles in slow rhythm against its side.

Hhhhooooom... hoo... hhhhooom...

The Hollow Thrum passed through trunks and into the dark.

The reply came slow. A half-thrum, short and expectant.

He crouched and drew the shared mark in the snow, slow and precise. Not his own clan's sign. Not theirs. The mark that said kin.

The reply returned, full this time.

They moved forward without hesitation.

The Gooseberry clan waited near a broken shelf of ice where water once fell. Now it hung still, jagged and pale like teeth frozen in place. Their territorial signal stood nearby: three spruce trunks bent to ground level, tips pointing toward the ledge. They were taller than Aluk's clan, with long, heavy arms built for climbing and hair the color of river stone and ash. Their elder was a wide-shouldered female with pale eyes and a twisted foot. She stood higher than the rest, breath deep and raspy.

The five approached and shared what had to be seen. One stepped forward and cast the image. The Sanctuary broken. Young scattered beneath branches. Injured dragging themselves from thunder sticks. He showed the Elder falling, the last breath drawn in silence. Then the final image, the new one who had risen.

Aluk.

The Gooseberry elder narrowed her eyes. She grunted twice and rolled one shoulder. She had seen machines on the river's edge and heard the crack of thunder from far away. She struck her chest once, then pointed to six of her strongest. They came forward. They would go.

****

Rok led the group bound for Tettegouche higher. Their legs stretched across stone where bark was thin and wind cut through narrow trails. Bent cedar branches marked the border, each limb tied by woody vines into a half-circle gateway. Where the cedars ended, spruce tips bent into downward hooks that pointed toward hidden ledges. When the ground shifted and the trees opened into a talus field, they stopped.

Rok, first among the five-strong Devils Lake clan, drummed the Hollow Thrum into a wide flat trunk.

Hhhhooooom… hoo… hhhhooom…

The call echoed but returned wrong. Not a thrum. A short, sharp bark from the rocks above, then silence. The five waited.

A dark form crawled from stone, limbs tense, hair slick with damp. Yellow eyes studied them without a blink. He gave a clipped grunt, not welcome, a challenge. The five showed open hands and the shared mark. One tapped his chest once, raised three fingers in peace.

Another shape dropped behind them. Then a third. They were surrounded. The Tettegouche leader rattled clicks and guttural chatter, *no welcome here, why come.*

Rok cast the image of loss: Sanctuary ravaged, thunder sticks ripping flesh, the Elder's final breath.

The watcher hissed and slapped his own chest, anger bright. A fourth figure swept an arm, fingers pressed in refusal. Memory flared between the groups: seasons ago, during the mating cycle, Aluk's fury had nearly ended one of their females. They had not forgotten and would not stand beside him.

The five stayed still. No teeth were bared. No sound. Rok stepped forward once more and cast a single image: their clan buckling under thunder sticks, bodies shuddering as metal tore through hair and flesh.

The watchers stilled. Tension held like a tilted trunk ready to fall.

A young Tettegouche male broke it, giving a double grunt and stepping toward the five. Sharp clicks rattled between him and the elder. The old one slapped snow and snarled.

No. Not this war. Not now.

The young one watched Rok and the rest leave. He did not follow, yet his gaze stayed fixed as bent cedar limbs swayed in the wind.

****

The trail to Finland wound through water-laced snow and roots that tangled like resting serpents. Territory markers here were immense: black spruce trunks bent and pegged to the ground in X-shapes, each X facing the marsh interior. The ground beneath held ancient cold.

The Finland clan was largest in bulk, bodies broad and powerful, hair dark with lichen and patches of frozen mud. Their arms matched logs in girth, movements slower but certain. Eyes were small and dark, shaped for the dim under old trees. Feet spread wide, trained by muck and moss.

The five reached a twisted cedar woven into an arch, the clan's welcome marker, and sounded the thrum. This time, reply came strong and fast, rumbling from many chests. Finland warriors emerged from shadow, surrounding a clearing where roots formed a ring over firm ground.

They chattered and grunted, pressed hands to chests, scraped lines into snow, and cast visions of what was seen and what would come. They gestured broadly, pointing to sky and soil.

The Finland elder, his broad teeth worn with age, watched carefully, then stepped forward and pointed. They would send twenty of their warriors.

CHAPTER 3

Matto left the Sanctuary just after the others had gone, his stride purposeful as he crossed the frost-crusted earth. The snow had been falling fine and slow, dusting the trees and rocks like breath turned solid. Not deep enough to bury prints yet, but enough to hush the world. The morning air had a sharpness to it, one that clung to the skin and pulled tight at the lungs. It was a cold that signaled change.

Beside him moved Karra, one of the strongest females in the clan. She had not spoken much before their departure, but her readiness had been clear. When Aluk gave the order, she rose without question. Broad-shouldered and long-limbed, her black hair shimmered with threads of silver in the weak light.

Their path would take them north, farther than the others. Beyond the old ridge, past the split river, deep into the oldest part of the forest. There, where the trees grew tall and close, the northernmost clan made their home.

Matto knew the path well. Every few cycles the Sasquatch followed it in search of mates, and he had walked it many times before. The last journey had been peaceful under the Elder's guidance. This time was different. This time war stalked his heels.

They moved without pause, their bodies blending into shadow and snow. The forest watched but did not stir. Crows above gave them space. Deer turned and vanished before them. Even the wind moved around them.

By midday, they had crossed the broken log bridge and reached the stretch where the birch trees grew in crooked lines. Karra paused here, sniffing the air.

She grunted softly. *Hairless ones.*

Matto crouched beside her. A thin trail of crushed grass and broken brush led along the slope. Footprints. Scent still fresh.

A sound ahead. A branch shifted.

Karra tensed. Her eyes narrowed. Her fingers brushed the ground near her feet, ready to spring.

Matto grunted sharply. *Negative. Not now. Not without the others.*

Karra hesitated, then nodded once. She understood.

They slipped into the thicker brush just as three hairless ones walked past, unaware. Wrapped in cloth and rubber, they carried thunder sticks, unaware of the eyes watching them from the dark forest.

Matto waited until they were gone. Then rose.

Their success relied on gathering as many of their kind as possible and they couldn't afford to get distracted.

Shortly after, the scent of fresh blood drifted through the birches, copper-rich on the cold air. A deer lay collapsed near a stump, flank torn open and steaming. Karra's head lifted. From the treeline three wolves emerged, shoulders low, hackles high, eyes shining with hunger. Four more shapes circled behind, forming a crescent that blocked the path north.

Karra stepped forward, silent challenge in her stance. The largest wolf bared its teeth and crawled closer, breath fogging.

Matto saw the tension in her frame. He wrapped one massive hand around the deer's neck, lifted the carcass with a wet slurp of sinew, and heaved it across a clearing. Meat and snow thudded together. Then he slammed both fists into the frozen ground. The boom rolled through the trees, shaking powder from limbs.

The wolves flinched. Hunger wrestled with instinct. The alpha gave a wary glance, then trotted after the carcass. One by one the others followed, vanishing into the shadows.

Karra's gaze lingered on the fading shapes. She gave Matto a short nod, respect in the gesture. Strength could be quiet.

The next two days were harder. The land grew steeper and colder. Snow deepened, biting at exposed skin while softening their steps. They crossed rivers hidden beneath ice and passed the moss-coated ribs of an old wooden structure.

Wildlife stirred here. Moose scraping bark. Lynx darting through the forest. Karra raised her chin, scenting the air, but they were not a threat. Not much native to the forest was.

On the third morning, the trees changed. The forest signaled the border long before any scent reached their noses. Massive spruce trunks had been bent into repeating arches, each arch laced with stripped saplings that pointed toward the clan's heartland. Some arches bore spiral twists, others ended with slanted cross-branches; the pattern told travelers how far they had come and which trails remained safe. No other clan used such intricate latticework, and any Sasquatch who saw it understood at once that the northern giants watched these paths.

They entered a grove where bark hung thick and dark, where the snow clung to every limb. The wind barely moved. The silence here was different. Watchful and untrusting.

Matto lifted his chin and gave the Hollow Thrum, a deep vibration in his chest that rippled into the still air. A peace-call. An old one.

They waited.

From above, a branch creaked. Then another. Shapes shifted among the trees.

The northern clan revealed themselves.

Three figures dropped from the limbs without sound. Their hair was darker, thicker, braided with bits of pine and stone. Their limbs longer, hands wider. They did not move like Matto's clan. They moved like wind, fast and quiet and precise.

One stepped forward. Not the largest, but clearly the leader. He grunted, a series of low tones, not unfriendly but firm.

Matto responded, casting an image to their minds. The battle. The fallen. The Elder crushed beneath Aluk's hand. The blood. The thunder sticks. The need for more.

The leader's eyes narrowed. He responded with an image of his own. Their sanctuary surrounded. Young ones hiding in hollow trees. Snow soaked in red.

Matto waited.

Another grunt. Not refusal. Not yet.

Then a fourth figure dropped from the trees. Taller than all of them. Scarred across one side. His grunts were quick and sharp. Karra bristled.

Matto stepped forward.

The new one did not speak in images. He used old words, gesture-heavy and direct.

"We have lost too. But we do not call others to die for our mistakes."

Matto did not flinch. He showed them another image. The numbers of the hairless ones. The machines. The thunder sticks. The spreading lines of paths and cutting tools.

Silence.

Then a slow response from the leader. He showed an image of branches snapping, of hairless ones falling, then the northern warriors standing tall over the bodies.

If we fight, the leader chattered, *we fight our way.*

Matto nodded.

They would not send many. But they would send their strongest.

With a final nod, the northern Sasquatch vanished back into the trees as if the meeting had never happened.

Matto and Karra turned south.

Four days after leaving, they returned to the Sanctuary. Snow fell again as they approached, thicker now, blanketing the stones and branches. Tracks filled the ground. Many tracks. The others had returned.

Karra stepped into the clearing without hesitation.

It was beginning.

CHAPTER 4

The sanctuary pulsed with life again. It buzzed with tension, thick with the knowledge of what was coming. Anticipation clung to the air. Muscles tensed, breath came short, eyes stayed watchful. The males stood taller, shoulders squared, their movements sharper. Young ones sensed the change and kept close to their mothers.

Aluk stood near the mouth of the cave, his breath slow, his broad chest rising and falling beneath thick hair that glistened with frost. One eye stared from beneath a swollen brow, the other ruined from his battle with the Elder. The wound remained dark, still healing. He carried it like a mark of rule, a token of blood-claim. Around him, the wounded stayed within the inner sanctuary, tended to by the females.

They came slowly. In small groups at first, emerging from the forest like shifting shadows, thick arms, heavy steps, deep-set eyes scanning the terrain with caution. Aluk's own kin, fifteen of them willing to drive the hairless ones back, watched from the edges of the clearing.

From Gooseberry came the first arrivals. Lean and fast, their hair streaked with rust and ash from the iron-soaked soil of their home. They moved with quick purpose, heads turning, sniffing the air. They gave the Hallow Thrum, the peace-call, and were answered. They crossed into the clearing with low chattering sounds, offering no threat.

The twenty from Finland came next. Their limbs were long, movements cautious and their hair slightly paler than the others. Snow clung to their shoulders and backs. They did not approach quickly, instead circling wide before settling along the outer edges of the sanctuary. Their silence spoke their hesitation.

Last came the ones from the north.

Twenty-two warriors emerged without sound, and their size dwarfed the others. Shoulders wide as tree trunks. Thick hair the color of stone and night. Their feet were broad, leaving deep marks in the snow. Eyes watched from beneath heavy brows, unblinking. They did not need to grunt to make their presence known. The earth seemed to tilt with their arrival.

Aluk stepped forward, his one good eye burning with focus.

He turned slowly, arms outstretched, sending a deep series of grunts that rippled across the air like rolling thunder. He paused, then cast an image into their minds. His memory filled the clearing, a vision of the ravine, the bodies of their kind lying broken in red-streaked snow. Thunder sticks. Screaming metal. The old one, lifeless beneath the trees.

The call echoed in every chest.

This was not just to strike back. It was to stop the taking. To end the noise. The stink of fire and metal. The tearing away of trees and quiet.

The Gooseberry clan beat their chests in rhythm. The Finland clan gave no signal, only watched. The northern ones stood like stone, unmoved, waiting.

One of the Finland group stepped forward. A tall male with pale eyes and long arms. He gave no call, but cast a small image. A burned clearing, ash still falling. A young one gone. Carried by hairless ones. It lingered, then faded.

He stepped back. Their answer was silence. Not refusal. But no promise.

Aluk grunted once in acknowledgment.

From the edge of the trees, the leader of the northern clan stepped forward. His body taller than Aluk's. A thick braid of hair hung over his left shoulder, with small bones tied into it. He spoke with no image, only grunts, deep and slow.

They had come. Not for Aluk. Not for his words. But for what had been done.

Aluk lowered his arms, accepting that truth.

He stepped back, raised both arms high again, and let out a long call that echoed into the trees. The clans joined him, each voice rising until the forest itself trembled. Excited chatter followed in surging waves.

Then silence.

There were now seventy-eight to stand with him.

Aluk's grunts came low but firm.

"We feed tonight. Tomorrow night, we rise."

CHAPTER 5

The Duluth Conference Center was beaming with activity as vendors prepared for Squatchsota, the country's largest Sasquatch-themed convention where cryptid fans gathered to celebrate, swap stories, and sell everything from casts of alleged footprints to hand-carved sculptures.

Randy Jackson sat on a folding stool behind their booth, sipping on a warm cup of coffee. He watched the other vendors set up around them, banners stretched overhead, plastic tubs opened with the resistance of tight seals, long tables being dressed in brown and green cloths printed with cryptid patterns.

"Think it looks good, Dad?"

Jenny stepped back with her hands on her hips, her sleeves dusted with fine bits of wood from the last sculpture she'd helped unpack. Her brown hair was pulled into a loose braid that kept falling over her shoulder.

Randy squinted at the setup. "Well, either the table's leaning or I am."

Jenny gave the edge a quick nudge with her boot. "It's not leaning. You're on uneven carpet."

He leaned forward and tapped one of the small cedar carvings lined up near the edge. "The big guy's looking smug. Hope he sells before he starts charging rent."

Jenny laughed. "He will. Besides, you put that smugness there."

Randy grinned. "Can't blame me, that's what Gus here asked for." He ran a hand over the sculpture's head. The Sasquatch's face was carved with care, each line in the brow and cheek considered, the thick hair etched with the same patience he gave to every piece.

This was their first time at Squatchsota, and the anticipation in the air buzzed like a trail-cam catching its first Bigfoot. They'd done roadside shows, pop-up markets, and a few cryptid-themed festivals back in Utah, but nothing like this. Not the big leagues. This was Duluth in December, and it was all the cryptid community could talk about.

Randy had spent months hunched over his garage workbench, working past midnight while he shaped cedar blocks into shaggy silhouettes and polished resin casts until his fingertips went numb. The shelves filled, then overflowed, and still he kept carving, worried they would not carry enough stock for the big event.

While sawdust drifted through the garage like wood-scented snow, Jenny ran the front end. She built a website from scratch, photographed every new sculpture, and answered late-night emails from podcast hosts and vloggers who wanted bespoke pieces. Orders trickled in at first, then grew as word spread through the cryptid fandom. Forums posted unboxing photos. A video review hit fifteen thousand views. By the time they packed the van for Minnesota, their mailing list was longer than Randy's tool pegboard.

Jenny reached for the small chalkboard sign, updating the prices with a smooth hand. "You sure these aren't too low?"

"They're just right. First impressions count more than dollars today."

She looked over at him. "Since when?"

"Since we started carving things with teeth and selling them to people who sleep with motion sensors in their backyard."

Jenny grinned and went back to writing. "Point taken."

A few booths down, someone fumbled a stack of T-shirts and let out a barked curse. The sound echoed faintly through the hall.

From where Randy sat, he could see the treeline of the Superior National Forest in the distance through the high front windows. Dark, sprawling woods pressed against the edge of the parking lot, separated from the conference center only by a narrow stretch of chain-link fence and a two-lane road.

"Morning!" a cheerful voice called from across the walkway. A tall woman with dark hair, high cheekbones and a quick smile approached their booth, balancing a half-unpacked crate on one hip and a display rack in her free hand.

Jenny turned. "Hi there!"

"I'm Lyneve. Just across the aisle from you. Wanted to say welcome before it gets too hectic."

"Thanks," Jenny said, smiling. "It's our first Squatchsota."

"Good year to start. This one always sells out fast. You'll go home with no stock left."

Randy stood slowly and rubbed the small of his back. "Looks like you've got good energy," he said. "Your booth's already got some life to it."

Lyneve laughed. "That's a first. Usually I'm still unboxing when the first guest shows up. I'll try to live up to the compliment."

Jenny tucked her chalk marker back into the toolkit. "What are you selling?"

"Leather goods mostly. Some journals, straps, pouches. All cryptid-themed."

"Sounds great," Randy said. "We'll come check it out once we're all set up."

"Looking forward to it." Lyneve smiled again and continued down the line.

Randy watched her go, then looked over at Jenny. "Nice lady. I give her two hours before she outsells us."

Jenny chuckled. "Only if her stuff smells like cedar and stares at you when you walk by."

He picked up one of the smaller figures and adjusted it on

the table. "Think we're ready?"

Jenny gave the booth another once-over. The lifelike Sasquatch carvings were arranged in groups, some mid-stride, others crouched in thoughtful poses, one towering over the rest with its arms raised as if about to bellow. Their display banner hung clean and straight, the logo centered and visible from halfway across the room.

Jenny stepped beside Randy to survey their neatly arranged tables. "We're ready," she said. "Now we just wait for the fanatics."

Randy checked his watch. "Gonna be a while. Six hours before doors open, at least," he said with a shrug. "Let's go for a walk and grab some lunch."

Jenny grinned. "Works for me."

Across the room, more vendors arrived, filling the air with friendly greetings, staple guns and the rustle of plastic wrap being torn from boxes. Somewhere behind the main hall, a forklift beeped in reverse as a stack of foldable chairs was delivered to the auditorium.

They drifted down the center aisle, weaving around half-built displays and open cartons. Vendors nodded greetings as they sorted banners, tablecloths and bins of plush cryptids. Randy paused to admire a table piled with laser-etched wooden maps of hidden lakes and rumored sighting spots, then strolled on. Jenny kept pace, eyes on everything.

"You think they're real?" she asked, lowering her voice while they passed a rack of glow-in-the-dark footprint casts.

Randy glanced at a fiberglass Yowie head mounted on the booth wall. "What, Sasquatch?"

"Yeah."

He shrugged, running his thumb over a resin bookmark shaped like a claw. "I figure something is out there. Whether it looks like the one I carve, who knows."

They stepped aside as two cosplayers rolled in a plywood mock-up of a research trailer. Jenny's gaze slid toward the hall's tall windows, where the tree line showed through frosted glass. "Wouldn't it be wild if one showed up here some year?"

Randy barked a laugh, steering her around a stack of tote boxes. "If a real one walked in, half these folks would beg for a selfie before they ran."

Jenny grinned at the image while they moved on, the low chatter of vendors and the rustle of unpacked merchandise following them down the row.

CHAPTER 6

The Duluth International Airport hummed with muted chatter and the soft scuff of boots on tile. Leon Scheppink tugged his wool-lined hood over his head and stepped outside after seventeen bleary hours of planes and layovers from the Netherlands. The cold slapped him awake, air so crisp it sliced straight through the fog of travel and cleared his thoughts.

Behind him, Wayne Picknell emerged with a grunt, hauling a duffel bag over one shoulder and blinking through the fine snow.

"I still can't believe I let you talk me into this. I've traded rain for snow," Leon said, watching flakes drift past the airport overhang.

Wayne let the bag drop and rolled his shoulders. "Dragged you halfway across the globe for the holy grail of cryptid conventions. You'll thank me once the vendor tables open and someone hands you a plaster cast of a three-toed footprint."

"Cryptids fascinate me, sure, but we could be in Australia right now with our wives soaking up the sun." Leon said as he looked out to the snow-covered cars in the parking lot.

Wayne grinned and pointed toward the taxi stand. "Let's just make it to the hotel first. My knees are negotiating a ceasefire."

"Besides, where else can you talk about Sasquatch for three days and no one calls you mad?"

Leon rolled his eyes. "In my house. We do it all the time."

They stepped outside, their breath curling in front of them like lazy smoke trails. The snow hadn't let up since they landed, and a thin layer already dusted their coats. A cab waited at the curb, engine running, lights glowing in the haze. The driver loaded their bags while Wayne climbed in slowly, mumbling about knees and the betrayal of time.

Their hotel sat on the eastern edge of Duluth, close to the forested sprawl that separated the city from Superior National Forest.

They had already passed three drive-through burger

joints and a pair of neon-lit chicken places. Leon tapped the window. "So many fast-food spots," he said, turning to Wayne. "One of these nights I want proper American barbecue, the slow-smoked kind. Brisket, ribs, pulled pork, the works."

"Deal," Wayne replied. "Find us a pit-stop that does burnt ends and I'm there."

Leon watched a pickup truck try and fail to make it up a slick incline, tires spinning before the driver gave up and rolled back down. Leon chuckled.

"This place is going to eat me alive," he said.

"You'll be fine," Wayne replied. "You're Dutch, you can survive anything."

They arrived at the hotel a few minutes later, the building modest but clean, with heavy timber accents and a front entry already marked by boot tracks. Leon pushed the doors open and let Wayne inside first, heat spilling out over them.

At the front desk, a young woman in a navy vest and ponytail greeted them with a bright smile.

"Welcome to Cascade Point Lodge," she said. "Checking in?"

Wayne nodded and leaned on the counter. "Picknell and Scheppink, thanks."

She scanned her screen. "Ah, yes. Two rooms for the weekend. You're here for Squatchsota, I'm guessing?"

Leon raised an eyebrow. "That obvious?"

She laughed. "You and everyone else. We're fully booked. The whole area is packed. This is our busiest weekend of the year."

Wayne beamed. "That's what I like to hear. Tell me, are the guests more the serious researcher types, or the ones wearing Bigfoot slippers and drinking from hairy coffee mugs?"

"A bit of both," she said. "We've got a guy with a taxidermy setup on the second-floor and a woman who claims she's seen the same one while camping in six different states."

Leon handed over a credit card. "Sounds like we're in for a colorful weekend."

"I'd say so," she replied, passing them their keys. "Conference Center is just across the road. Easiest walk in Duluth, unless it ices."

Wayne leaned on the counter. "We brought boots and an unreasonable amount of enthusiasm."

She laughed. "You'll fit right in."

The elevator chimed as it opened. They stepped in, and as the doors shut, Wayne looked over at Leon.

"See? You're smiling already."

"I'm just thinking how you tricked me into this," Leon said. "And how it'll probably end with me buried in souvenir T-shirts and conversations about tree knocks."

Wayne grinned. "Better than spending December in a suit."

Once in their adjoining rooms, they unlatched the connecting door and left it half-open so conversation could drift between beds. Wayne tossed his coat onto the nearest chair and eased down with a satisfied sigh. "Well. This is it. My cryptid pilgrimage begins."

Leon dropped his bag by the closet. "Nap time for you. I'm going to stretch my legs."

Wayne raised an eyebrow. "Is this that jet-lag optimism kicking in?"

Leon zipped up his coat again and smiled. "Maybe. Or

maybe I just want to see the trees."

"Don't get lost," Wayne called as Leon shut the door behind him.

Leon waved without turning and made his way out through the side entrance. The snow was still falling, though the wind had picked up a bit. He pulled his scarf tighter and walked along the cleared sidewalk, following the curve of the road east before veering off toward a small trail entrance marked by a wooden sign and a chain-link divider meant to keep vehicles out.

This close to the edge of the forest, the air carried a different quality, denser, quieter, filled with the hush of falling snow and the subtle creak of heavy branches. Leon stepped onto the trail, noting how the snow had blanketed everything into muted shapes. Footprints from earlier walkers had already begun to fade beneath the fresh layer. The path curled forward, deeper into the trees.

Back inside, Wayne was already half-asleep with the TV on low, snuggled under the covers.

CHAPTER 7

James Jackson sat on the porch with a chipped mug of black coffee steaming in his hands. The wind stirred through the skeletal branches around his property, carrying the distant sound of a snowplow from the main road.

His land stretched just shy of the eastern forest line, less than half a mile from the edge of the city and whatever fool circus was setting up over at the conference center. Bigfoot fanatics in shaggy costumes or decked out in head to toe camo. He had noticed the banners and signs for Squatchsota and knew the type who flocked to it.

He sipped slowly, eyes scanning the treeline beyond his split-rail fence. Chickadees darted between the feeder and the eaves, ignoring the rusted truck parked at the side of the shed.

Hand-painted boards hung along his fence, each one

shouting: KEEP OUT, OWNER ARMED, NO WARNINGS.

"Whole damn world's gone soft," he mumbled, setting the mug down beside him. "Talkin' about squatch-men like they're fairy tale creatures instead of what they truly are. Walkin', breathin', killin' machines."

His boots creaked against the boards as he stood and stretched, joints popping like gravel under a tire. He shuffled down the steps, gloved hands tightening around the collar of his coat as he made his way to the side yard. A fresh row of claymore mines lay just inside the property's edge, half-buried and wired to a battery pack he checked every morning.

He passed the third one, gave it a quick toe nudge.

"Still hot," he said with a grunt of approval. "You don't cross James Jackson's line unless you plan on leavin' a piece of yourself behind."

He walked the perimeter like he did every afternoon, eyes peeled for tracks. Snow showed everything if you knew what to look for. Rabbits mostly. One fox print. Deer used to come through all the time, sometimes in groups of six or seven. Now, nothing. They knew what was really out there. Or they'd been taken.

James reached the back edge of the property, where his

chain-link fence met the woods, and leaned against the post. Beyond it, trees thickened, crowding the space with shadow and cold.

"I know you're still out there," he said softly, not to the woods but to whatever moved inside them. "Think you can wait me out. You can't. Ain't goin' nowhere."

He stood a moment longer, unmoving, then spat into the snow and turned back for the house.

Inside, the living room was dark except for the glow of a small TV set playing an old western. He kept it on for the noise. He didn't watch much anymore. The recliner had a quilt draped over it, faded from years of wear. A rifle rested against the wall near the back door, barrel oiled and clean. An M16 leaned beside the front door within arm's reach.

James crossed to the dim corner of the living room, where a metal shelf held four trail-cam monitors, a stack of SD cards, and a pair of battered binoculars. He tapped a button to cycle through the frozen feeds, then flipped open the notepad lying beside the screens, its pages filled with crude sketches and dates. Running a finger down the last column, he mumbled, "December 1. Cold snap. No prints since the thirteenth. No howls either. They ain't gone. They're planning something."

He closed the notepad and looked out the window again. Past the shed. Toward the slope where the trees came closest.

The woods were quiet. Too quiet. Nature didn't go silent without a reason.

Somewhere in town people were stringing up banners and stacking books on folding tables. Folks laughing about eight-foot beasts and plaster casts while he sat with mines in the snow.

"Let 'em laugh," he said under his breath. "One day they'll learn."

The sun dipped behind the trees, throwing soft bands of blue and white across the yard. He made one last round before dusk, slower this time, listening for the wrong kind of silence.

They would come back soon.

He could feel it.

And he always trusted his gut.

He had ever since Vietnam.

CHAPTER 8

The drywall job had run long. Michael Hoffman wiped his hands on a crumpled rag and slid into the driver's seat of his truck. His phone buzzed before he could turn the key.

"Hey Dad," came his son's voice. "Pete's going crazy again. He won't stop barking."

Michael leaned back with a tired sigh. "Is he at the back fence?"

"Yeah. Growling at the trees again. You want me to bring him in?"

"Yeah. I'm heading home now. Be there in twenty."

He hung up and started the engine. The low rumble echoed off the nearby metal buildings, all washed in the soft light of late afternoon. There had been brief flurries of snow drifting through the air on and off during the day, never sticking for long but reminding him winter was here. The sun was dropping fast. Another half hour and it would be gone, leaving the sky cold and bruised. He did not like the timing. Something about that dog's barking had carried a sharper edge lately.

He pulled onto the road, his truck clunking into gear, and settled into the silence. The heater coughed before warm air reached his boots. The drive home was short, fifteen minutes when traffic cooperated, cutting through the quiet edges of Duluth where houses gave way to tree lines and unlit stretches of land opened wide and wild.

Michael's house sat midway along the narrow street, just shy of the thicker forests to the east. From his back porch you could see the first shadows of Superior National Forest, a treeline that started neat and then swallowed the land in rough layers. About three hundred yards farther, the trees merged into dark nothing.

He eased the truck into the driveway, let the engine idle for a moment, then shut it off. When he stepped out, the stillness wrapped around him. No wind, no traffic hum, no neighbor outside. Instinct sharpened. Years of military patrols had trained him to recognize the wrong kind of quiet, a hush that hangs like a held breath before trouble breaks.

He walked toward the backyard and stopped halfway along the path. The swing set sat as a weak outline, the garden darker still, yet not a branch creaked. The silence raised the hair on his neck. He waited, listening for any shuffle in the brush. Nothing.

"Dad?" Adam's voice called from the side door.

Michael pivoted and headed that way. His son had already cracked the door open, head poking out into the dim porch light.

"Pete's inside. He stopped barking about five minutes ago."

Michael exhaled and nodded. "Thanks, buddy. Anything else?"

Adam shook his head. "Nah."

Michael stepped inside and glanced toward the back of the house. Pete was lying by the sliding glass door, ears up but still.

Michael dropped his gear by the door and crossed to the glass. He looked out.

He narrowed his eyes.

Something didn't sit right. The trees didn't just look still, they looked… wrong. Like a painting. Perfect. Motionless. And watching.

He slid the door open just an inch. Cold air slipped in. Pete stood and let out a low growl. Nothing loud, just enough to confirm Michael wasn't imagining things.

Michael stepped out slowly. The deck creaked under his weight. The cold bit through his flannel shirt and settled deep in his spine.

He stared into the woods.

Nothing.

But it wasn't just quiet. It was vacant. The animals were gone. No deer. No squirrels. Not even a bird taking off in the distance.

He scanned the ground. The snow between the yard and the tree line was mostly untouched, save for a few sets of old deer prints near the far left fence post. And yet, the stillness pushed against him.

He turned to the dog. "What is it, boy?"

Pete didn't bark. He didn't move either. Just kept staring.

Michael looked back out. Whatever had stirred the dog was still there. Somewhere beyond the shadows, beyond the frost and pine.

He stood there for another minute, his brow low. Then he stepped back inside and locked the door. He gave the glass one last look before pulling the curtain across and telling Pete to go join the kids.

His phone buzzed again.

"Work tomorrow?" It was from a buddy asking about a side job.

Michael stared at the message for a second before typing back, "Maybe."

He didn't like maybes. But tonight, something in the air made him uneasy. He didn't know what it was. Only that the forest wasn't quiet in the way it should be.

It was watching.

CHAPTER 9

Aluk stood near the front of the great cave, where the stone sloped wide and low, opening onto the forest below. His eye scanned the gathering beneath, his large frame still, breath steady. The wound from the Elder's final strike had long since scabbed, but the pain had not vanished. He carried it like he carried the memory of that fight, close and layered with heat and certainty.

They had come.

Clans from the deep thickets of Finland State Forest and the snow-slick heights near Gooseberry Falls. The largest clan from the northern edge of Superior National Forest had arrived last, their numbers greater than any others. Tall, broad creatures with long, dark hair, and solemn expressions. They spoke little, kept together, but they had come. Aluk had counted them all. Fifty-eight willing to move with him. Added to his own, seventy-three would strike.

Only one clan had refused. He did not speak their name.

The warriors shifted and chattered in the snow-packed clearing, their hairy bodies steaming in the cold. Grunts and light chest thumps passed between them, eyes flashing beneath heavy brows. Some stood no taller than six of the hairless one's feet, others rose as high as eleven. A rough, living wall of muscle, instinct and memory.

Aluk stepped onto the ledge above them. His thick fingers raised, then curled tight. A hush swept the gathering.

He let the moment stretch, watching them.

Aluk grunted low, chest vibrating in a silent drum. The front rows leaned closer, bodies tilting in unison, awaiting his signal.

He pressed a fist to his chest and released, claws spread wide. His deep, guttural clicks punctuated each gesture, translating to meaning only kin could understand. Then he cast the image.

Into their minds flowed the memory. The Elder, rigid and still, throat crushed in a final gasp. The circle of shocked kin standing around him. The instant when Aluk took the place beside the bowing trees by delivering the strike that ended the Elder's life.

Aluk lowered his hand to his side and released a low rumble. With another sweep of fingers and a curl of his palm, he conveyed loss.

He kept our ancient ways. His clicks hinted. *He guided us beneath forest shadows.* Each guttural syllable matched the motion. *While the hairless ones hacked great trees, poisoned winding streams, hunted our young.*

A tall female on the edge of the Finland group rumbled her approval and pounded a fist against her thigh. A wave of sharp clicks ran through the gathering, brief, breathless chatter.

Aluk leaned forward, brows drawn. With a single, forceful grunt he shared the next vision.

They came with thunder sticks. His clicks echoed. The image flashed: thunder ripping through underbrush, black sticks spitting death. *They stole half our breathers. Mothers. Young. The forest floor still reeks with their blood.*

He straightened and began to pace, each step marking intention, arms hanging loose, gaze hard as frozen streams. *We have hidden too long.* The growl rolled from his chest. His open palm swept in a gathering motion. *Now we walk into their world. And we take, just like they did.*

From the side, Matto moved into the clearing. He let out two low hoots that trembled through chests, then pressed fingertips to his heart. His return from the north meant their largest clan now formed a living barrier behind him.

Aluk inclined his head toward the treeline. Three scouts crouched near the snow-lipped edge, bodies as still as winter stands.

I sent path-seekers. His guttural hiss pulsed through the group. *They found the hidden trails from forest to dens.* His clawed hand swept toward a distant glow on the horizon.

A ripple of low chatter answered him. Some warriors gripped their arms, hands curling, eyes bright with hunger.

Aluk opened both hands, rising on the balls of his feet, claws parted like brambles ready to strike. His chest heaved. *We do not hunt for hunger.* His clicks sent shivers along spines. *We do not move for joy.* He let the silence settle like fresh snow, heartbeats thrumming in the hush.

Then a single grunt, slow and resonant.

We move for breathers who no longer walk. He tapped his chest, then swept his fingers across his throat. *For young ones buried beneath cold dirt.* His palm brushed the ground. *For streams that taste of poison.*

No words followed, only the deep thumping of limbs drumming against snow. He let them feel the mourning, the anger, the relentless purpose.

Then he raised his voice, a rumble that cracked like falling timber.

We scatter their bones.

A chorus of growls rose, layered and deep, echoes of distant howls stirring the frosty air.

Aluk waited until the last echo faded, then tapped a single finger against his palm, commanding silence. *We move in darkness.* His low hiss carried. *From the treeline. They will see no rise of steam or hear us coming. We move as one.*

He faced the entire gathering and, with one powerful stroke of his hand, shared the final edict.

Break all. Spare none.

A charged hush fell, the forest bracing for what came next.

Then Aluk took the first step forward.

The clearing erupted. Chatter became roars, low and primal. Some slammed fists into trees, others pounded the ground with open palms. A few struck trunks in rhythmic bursts with knuckles. The sound rolled across the snow, into the forest, a wave of fury and purpose rising beneath the frozen sky.

Far off among the trees, the scouts remained hidden, already watching the paths ahead.

CHAPTER 10

"Leon, for the love of all that is mildly interesting, will you please hurry up?" Wayne's voice echoed from the hallway outside their hotel room, thick with British irritation. "I've already tied my shoes, untied them, tied them again, and I've memorized half the vending machine options."

Inside the room, Leon stood by the mirror, adjusting the collar of his coat. "You've dragged me halfway around the world, and now you want to sprint? Give a man ten minutes to recover from jet-lag."

Wayne huffed. "Recovery's for after the event, not before. I didn't come all this way to miss the first whiff of beef jerky and bad taxidermy."

Leon stepped out, a beanie tucked under one arm, expression calm as ever. "Have I ever told you you're a strange man?"

Wayne grinned. "Only about a hundred times."

As they prepared to leave, Leon paused in the doorway. "Do you have our lanyards with the tickets in them?"

Wayne's brow furrowed. "No. You were supposed to get them."

Leon huffed and turned on his heel, marching back into the room while Wayne waited in the hallway.

A moment later Leon re-emerged, lanyards dangling from his coat pocket. He stepped past Wayne and together they followed the hallway to the lobby. When they pushed through the doors into the frigid night air, Wayne shivered and mumbled, "Bloody hell, it's cold enough to wake the dead."

Leon zipped his collar higher and grinned. "Keep it down, mate. My mother-in-law will claw her way up here asking why we never visit."

The large conference center across the road loomed, its entry banners catching the glow from overhead lights. A digital sign blinked above the main doors: *Welcome to Squatchsota – Sasquatch Summit.*

They stepped into the street, Leon not-so-subtly reminding Wayne to look the right way before oncoming headlights arrived. As they walked through the parking lot, a few attendees were still setting up inside, the event not officially open for another thirty minutes. Trucks idled nearby, vendors unloading bins of merchandise and life-size cardboard cutouts.

Leon watched a vendor pull a large wooden crate off the back of a trailer and drop it directly on his foot. The man let out a string of frustrated grunts before hobbling off. Wayne raised an eyebrow. "I think we just witnessed the first casualty of the weekend."

"Wooden foot for a wooden Bigfoot," Leon mumbled.

They reached the glass doors where a jovial man behind a small desk grinned wide. Wayne's lanyard hung around his neck as he stepped forward and held it out. The man scanned the badge, then pointed to Leon. "And you, my friend?" He tapped his own lanyard to the scanner.

Leon mimicked the gesture. The man chuckled and waved them inside. "Enjoy Squatchsota, guys."

Warm air, fragrant with rich food and coffee, filled the room. They walked slowly past the booths in mid-setup. Folding tables, handwritten signs, bins of fur-patterned hats, and racks of T-shirts covered with bold block letters. Some said Believe, others had silhouettes of towering ape-like creatures stalking tree lines.

They passed a large banner hanging from the ceiling, pointing to the concession area. Wayne stopped, inhaled deeply, and licked his lips. "Damn, that smells good. But first we mingle."

They approached a booth decorated in deep brown tones, with a banner that read *The Sasquatch Artisan*. Behind it stood Randy, hunched slightly with age, carefully arranging a wooden sculpture on a cloth-draped riser. Beside him, his daughter Jenny stacked business cards beside a row of carved figurines.

Randy looked up and smiled. "Evenin' fellas."

Wayne's eyes beamed. "These are bloody fantastic."

"Thank you kindly," Randy said, brushing sawdust off his flannel sleeve. "Been carving critters since before my daughter here could spell Sasquatch."

Jenny smiled warmly. "He's not kidding. We've been doing booths out west, Utah, and Nevada mostly, but this is our first time in Duluth."

Leon leaned in to study a six-inch tall statue. The detail

in the brow ridges and fingers was startling. "That's a fine hand."

Randy chuckled. "Don't look too close. I carved that one while half-frozen in a shed, power out and fingers stiff."

Wayne nodded. "Makes it authentic. I'll be back later to grab one before the crowd tramples everything."

As they continued down the row, a mannequin from one of the booths suddenly tipped sideways. A woman scrambled to catch it, but it slid right into Leon's path and smacked him in the knee.

"Oi," he mumbled, steadying the fake Bigfoot torso. "That's assault."

Wayne burst out laughing. "Leon, if that's the only Sasquatch that jumps you this weekend, I'll count us lucky."

Leon straightened the mannequin, patted its hairy chest, and said, "Easy, big fella. I'm just here to browse."

They walked on, Wayne already talking excitedly about the panel on alleged government cover-ups. Leon only half-listened, taking in the crowd and the flicker of anticipation in the air.

CHAPTER 11

The forest trembled beneath the charge.

Dozens of massive shapes tore through the undergrowth, their strides long, their movements thunderous but sure. Bark tore where hands brushed trees, snow lifted in powder clouds beneath thick feet. From six feet to eleven, the Sasquatch horde moved like one, pulsing toward the edge of the hairless one's dens.

At the front ran Aluk. His chest rose and fell steadily, breath curling in the cold as he led them through the narrowing trees. His hair clung to him, heavy with melting snow. He could feel the others behind him, feel the vibration of their steps carried in the earth and could smell the distant scent of hairless ones, sweet and bitter like rotting stone.

To the sides and behind him, the horde churned forward. Clans from the north, from the coast lands, from the deep bluffs near endless water. Some with hair as black as cave rock, others with pale hair like dry grass, and some with red streaks along their shoulders from clay-painted markings. They made no sound other than the rhythm of their movement.

In the trees above, birds clung to branches, unmoving. No chirps, no wings. Silence wrapped the woods like fog.

A fox crouched deep in its burrow and stayed hidden. A herd of deer, far off, bolted at once as the horde passed near. Even the squirrels stilled, tucked inside hollows. Every animal felt it. The wild knew to stay hidden.

Up ahead, the forest bent slightly, opening into a low ridge where two scouts crouched near a break in the trees. They stood still, half-shrouded in thickets, their bodies unreadable to the human eye. Not even the owls above would have seen them if not for the faint rise of their breath in the cold air.

Aluk lifted a hand, halting the mass behind him.

The horde stopped. Breath steamed upward. Eyes scanned the woods ahead.

The scouts stepped forward. One grunted low, spreading his hands and crouching. His movements were slow. He touched the ground, then pointed with two fingers toward the right, toward a long sloping trail that wrapped behind a row of human dens.

The other scout raised a hand, then flattened it and moved it forward, low to the ground. A crawl path, closer to the tree line, less snow, more shadows. He then indicated that fellow scouts miles away still watched each route, ready to signal any movement from the hairless ones.

Images formed in Aluk's mind, sent through brief bursts of chatter and gesture. The hairless ones were restless. Some were near the stone building with bright light and loud voices. Others moved along black paths, unaware how close they were to the Sasquatch's wrath.

Aluk stepped forward. He cast an image to those closest to him, a split of direction, three ways, like roots of a tree pushing through soil. The others saw what he meant. They passed it along. Grunts and low chatter moved through the crowd like a pulse.

He raised both arms, calling the moment.

To the left, he pointed. A group peeled off, their leader marked by a slash of old scar across the chest.

To the right, another group moved. Taller beasts, thick in the chest and arm, with longer strides, turned and vanished into the side woods.

The rest stayed with Aluk.

Aluk gave one short grunt, then another. The signal to move.

The woods filled again with motion, branches snapping, snow crushed under hundreds of feet.

Each group took its own path.

Some moved along half-frozen creeks, barely touching the icy water.

Some slid through dense brush, low to the ground, silent and unseen.

Others ran, broad strides carrying them fast through the narrowing spaces between forest and stone.

Aluk pressed forward, his eye catching flickers of white snow between trees, the dark shape of dens just beyond. His arms swung wide as he moved, his breath smooth. This ground would not belong to the hairless ones for much longer.

Behind him, the sounds of the clan were thunder on snow.

In the dark, all that could be seen of them were their eyes, glowing through the trees in shades of yellow, amber, and red.

CHAPTER 12

Wayne leaned against the wall beside the long window, rubbing at his hip with the side of his hand. The ache had crept in slow, then settled deep. He shifted his weight slightly, breathing through it, pretending it wasn't as bad as it was. Outside, the light snow came in slanted threads, thin and constant, catching in the glow of the parking lot lamps.

He watched a couple carrying tote bags make their way to the entrance, bundled tight, heads down against the cold. Another group stood by the curb, arguing playfully about whether to head back to the hotel for drinks or stay longer. Every few seconds, someone new came through the revolving doors, shaking snow off their coats and boots.

His eyes drifted past them, toward the tree line beyond the far side of the lot. It sat dark and still, hunched beneath the weight of winter. The edges of the branches blurred into the night. Wayne blinked. Something had moved.

It was quick, just a shift in the shape near the base of a tall pine. He narrowed his eyes, adjusting his stance slightly. Might have been the wind, might have been nothing.

The shape shifted again.

"I need to get my eyes checked. Been too long," he mumbled, straightening.

It was the damn conference again, all that chatter about sightings and blurry trail-cam shots. Wayne had been in Duluth less than a day and already the shadows felt busy. Bigfoot on the brain, as Leon liked to tease.

He turned to share the thought, but Leon was gone. The coffee stall where he had hovered a moment ago now stood empty.

Wayne glanced right and spotted a lanky teenager in a hoodie. He waved him over. "Hey, do you see anything out there?"

The boy stepped closer and pressed his face to the glass. "Nah, nothing. Just snow and headlights." He straightened and stuck out his hand. "I'm Zachariah."

Wayne clasped the hand and shook it, a polite smile softening his words. "Wayne Picknell. Flew in from the UK this morning."

Zachariah's eyebrows shot up. "That's epic. You here only for the festival?"

"Exactly. Dragged a mate along for company. We have been itching to check it out."

"I've lived here forever." Zachariah jerked a thumb toward the doors. "Mom's a cryptid nut, so we never miss Squatchsota. She'll be coming tomorrow. Had to work tonight."

"That is dedication."

"Come on." Zachariah nodded toward a nearby booth. "You gotta see these tracks. They found some up in Superior, another set by Gooseberry Falls, and even a bunch near the airport."

Wayne followed as Zachariah wove through the crowd. "Local prints, is it?"

"Yep. Pretty wild stuff." Zach's grin showed a chipped front tooth, evidence of teenage adventure. "Hey, did you catch the story about those campers up north?"

"Can't say I have. What happened?"

The boy's voice dropped to a conspiratorial whisper. "Group of friends went into Superior two weeks ago. Only one dude crawled out. Said Bigfoot tore the others up. People thought he was making it up, then one of the missing turned up alive after some specialist team rescued him. Everyone's freaking out."

Wayne's brows rose. "That only happened a fortnight ago?"

Zachariah blinked. "Fortnight? What's that?"

"Two weeks," Wayne said, giving a small shrug. "Sorry, old British habit."

"Got it," Zachariah said, eyes widening again. "Makes those prints feel a lot scarier, right?"

"Certainly raises the stakes. Cheers for the heads-up."

They reached the footprint display. Plaster casts sat on velvet pads while an older woman in camo pants gave her pitch.

"These were lifted last winter, twenty miles north of town, another near Gooseberry Falls, and two fresh sets beside the airport fence. The landowner caught them before the thaw."

Wayne studied a cast nearly two feet long, nails gouging deep grooves. Zach's eyes shone with wonder.

"That thing is massive," the teen breathed.

"Imagine meeting what made it," Wayne replied, hovering a fingertip above the glass.

"I run a cheap trail cam at my family cabin." Zach's voice held shy pride. "Nothing clear yet, but something big walked past it."

"Keep at it," Wayne encouraged. "Evidence turns up where you least expect it."

"Thanks, man." Zachariah gulped the last of his soda and drifted toward a monitor looping grainy night footage.

Wayne's hip ached, but he ignored it and scanned the hall until Leon reappeared near a rack of novelty Bigfoot suits, chatting with the camo-clad woman. Wayne eased through the crowd.

Onstage the emcee, Darryl Delgado, tapped the mic. "Our first talk begins soon. Find your seats."

Wayne and Leon settled halfway up the auditorium. Zachariah slipped into the row beside them, and a broad-shouldered stranger in hiking boots dropped into the seat next to Leon.

"Brad Samples," he said with a firm handshake. "Researcher from Tennessee. Half my life in the Smokies."

Leon returned the shake, dry humour in his tone. "Leon from the Netherlands. Tagged along with this lunatic Brit."

Wayne chuckled. "Wayne Picknell, pleased to meet you. Zachariah here is the hometown expert."

Zachariah lifted a hand. "Hey."

Brad grinned. "Good crew already. Nice break from talking to tree stumps in the dark."

Leon leaned toward him. "We head to Oregon on Monday, Bigfoot Center first, then down to Bluff Creek."

"Brilliant choice," Brad said. "Bluff Creek is sacred ground."

Delgado's voice carried over the PA. "Welcome to Squatchsota, the biggest cryptid gathering this side of the Mississippi. Whether you drove ten minutes or flew ten hours, we are thrilled you made it."

Applause rippled through the hall.

"Our first speaker needs no introduction," Delgado continued.

Steven Bengle strode onstage, confidence radiating with each step. He stacked a pile of books, straightened his jacket and flashed the audience a cheesy smile.

"As many of you know, I call Sasquatch the Friends of the Forest," he began, clicking to blurry photos. "They leave me baskets of nuts and mushrooms when I sing for them at dawn."

Coughs scattered through the rows. Leon mumbled to Wayne, "If the next speaker yodels about fairy rings, I am leaving."

Wayne smothered a laugh. "Hold out. The second talk should be worth the wait."

Brad nodded. "Gotta endure the show to get the substance."

When Bengle finally wrapped up and Delgado thanked him, the trio exchanged relieved looks while the lights dimmed for the next presentation.

CHAPTER 13

James Jackson sat in his lounge room, a half-eaten sandwich perched on the arm of his recliner, crumbs on his faded flannel shirt. The TV mumbled something from a rerun western, but he wasn't listening. His eyes kept drifting toward the window.

He didn't like how quiet it had gotten; a knot of anxiety tightened in his stomach.

Dusk glazed the yard in bruised violet and rust, the last smear of sunlight catching the treetops with dull gold. Thin flakes drifted sideways on a lazy wind, settling over the grass like white dust. A powdery mist hovered at the forest edge, turning the trunks into a wavering wall.

Then the sensor light beside the shed blinked on.

James didn't move. He waited, one hand slowly setting

the sandwich aside. He stood without a sound and walked to the window. Pulled the curtain just slightly, two fingers gripping the edge.

Something moved fast. Like a blur.

Too tall to be a man. Too broad. It disappeared into the edge of the yard before he could focus on detail. The shed stood about 150 yards away. That was his line. His warning marker. He'd wired the ground around it months ago, waiting for the opportunity.

He stepped back, heart beating fast but locked into a rhythm, and opened the hallway cabinet. The M16 hung inside, loaded and cleaned as always. Habit. Muscle memory. Vietnam had taught him that much.

Back at the window, he saw another figure slide between the trees, just on the border of where the light spilled out. This one moved slower, more cautious.

He grunted softly, more out of frustration than fear. "Should've figured you wouldn't come alone."

He knelt beside the couch, reached under, and pulled out a flat plastic box with a blinking green light. The remote. Four toggles, two safeties, and enough power wired in to rip a hole through anything unlucky enough to cross that yard. He flicked the cover and checked the readout. Still armed.

He rose, careful not to disturb the curtain again. They'd be watching too.

Hunching over the row of monitors, he watched and waited.

The first shape moved, crawling low on its belly across the snow like it had too many joints. The movement made James' skin want to crawl away without him.

The other hugged the far side of the shed.

He knew that ground. Knew the range. The first had just crossed the outer line. If they went two more yards, they'd be inside the kill zone.

The second one darted forward.

That was enough.

"I'm not letting you bastards get close to the house," James mumbled. "I'm gonna send you back to the hell you came out of."

He flipped both safeties, hit the toggles, and dropped to the floor.

The sound that followed rattled the picture frames on the walls. The back yard lit up in orange and gray, a flash brighter than the afternoon sun. The concussion shook the old cabin's bones. Shards of frozen earth exploded skyward. Then the silence came back, heavier than before.

He crawled up, M16 in hand, and peered through the now-cracked window. Smoke hung low. Splinters and charred snow scattered across the clearing. One form was motionless, lying half-tangled in the fence wire. The other twitched and dragged itself toward the treeline.

James moved.

He opened the back door, stepped out, the M16 up before his foot hit the porch boards.

The creature turned. One eye glowed amber. The other half of its face was ruined.

James didn't speak. He squeezed the trigger three times.

Three sharp cracks snapped across the yard.

The thing jerked once, then lay still.

For a long while, he didn't lower the rifle.

Then, finally, he exhaled. Cold breath steamed from his nostrils.

He looked at what was left of his yard.

The shed sat heavily damaged, its walls collapsed in

places while jagged beams still clung to the frame. Smoke curled upward from charred timbers in lazy ribbons.

Nothing moved in the trees.

No birds. No rustle. Not even the wind.

He mumbled to himself, "I warned you I would be ready."

Back inside, he shut the door, locked it, leaned the rifle against the wall. He passed the TV, still playing its western, the hero mid-gunfight with someone who wouldn't walk away.

He sat back in his chair. Looked at the sandwich.

He picked it up, finished it slowly, crumbs scattering across his lap.

Then he moved the plate aside and returned to the monitors.

And waited.

CHAPTER 14

Michael Hoffman had just finished putting the last plate in the cupboard.

Pete, their scrappy wire-haired Jack Russell with a bark bigger than his bite, stood frozen in the middle of the kitchen. His collar jingled faintly. Then he looked up.

Not at Michael.

At the back door.

Michael turned. "What's up, boy?"

Pete didn't bark. Didn't growl. Just stared, tail stiff, ears forward, body tense.

Then the sound of an explosion rolled across the neighborhood like a hammer to the chest.

Distant, but close enough to vibrate the window glass. The kids jumped. Pete barked at the back door like it had insulted him.

Michael froze for a second, listening. That wasn't a car backfiring. It wasn't fireworks either. It had a low, thudding belly to it. Something military.

"What was that?" Adam's voice cracked. His youngest started crying.

"I'm not sure, bud," Michael said as he made his way to the back door.

He looked out through the glass. Nothing.

Just snow dusting the grass. The tree line, about three hundred yards back, looked quiet. But it didn't feel right. The air had a pressure to it. A tension that whispered of things moving out there, just beyond sight.

He made his way to the front door. He turned the lock slowly, opening the door quietly.

The neighborhood had stirred.

Three houses down, someone was already out on their porch. His neighbor Linda was walking down her driveway in her robe with slippers on. He wanted to yell at her to get back inside, but the words caught in his throat.

Because something was coming.

Fast.

Monstrous.

A dark, wide shape, too large for a person and hunched with a predatory gait. It tore across the snow with impossible speed. Michael opened his mouth to yell but barely got a breath out before the thing reached her.

It hit her like a freight train. Tackling her to the ground and straddling her.

Then it started slamming her head against the pavement.

Again.

And again.

And again.

Michael staggered backward, heart hammering as disbelief burned behind his eyes. He closed the door with trembling hand and took several careful steps away, still reeling from what he had seen.

His lungs strained for air and he forced himself to take a

deep breath.

Then came the screaming.

High, ragged, some male, some female, all human and terrified. The sound of feet on pavement. Something heavy thudding. Car horns. More screaming.

Michael moved to the living room.

"Downstairs," Michael said to his kids. "Now. All of you."

He grabbed Pete by the collar, shoved open the basement door and pointed.

"Go. Don't argue. Take the dog."

The kids hesitated, but the look on their father's face shifted something in them. His eyes weren't questioning. They were already calculating. They bolted down the stairs.

Michael turned and moved into the hallway. He stopped at the tall cabinet, punched in the code, and the door clicked open. He pulled out the 12-gauge. Checked it. Loaded. Safety off.

He also grabbed the Winchester Model 70 and a box of .338 Win Mag. His hands shook as he checked the action and slammed the bolt shut.

From the back of the house, glass shattered.

The back sliding doors exploded inward, and something snarled loud enough to vibrate his ribs.

Michael spun toward the sound. The beast filled the doorway, massive and slouched, snow melting off dark hair, eyes lit like hot coals. It registered the rifle in his hands a split second before he squeezed the trigger.

The blast lit the room. The creature flinched, roared, and staggered, knocking over the dining room chairs.

He worked the bolt and fired again into its chest.

Still moving.

He stepped forward and fired once more, aiming for its face.

It collapsed. Slammed face down on the tile with a grunt that shook the floor. Its limbs twitched.

Michael didn't wait.

He ran for the hallway, grabbed the shotgun from the table, and turned sprinting to the basement door. He yanked it open, stepped through, and slammed it shut behind him before locking it.

He stood there, back against the door, heart pounding against his ribs like it wanted out.

Below, the kids were crying.

Adam looked up at him, wide-eyed.

"What happened?" he asked.

Michael looked at the rifle and shotgun in his hands. The sound of the creature still echoing in his ears.

He tried to speak.

"I... I don't know, son."

And then the floor creaked above them.

CHAPTER 15

They stepped out of the auditorium, still singing the praises of the last presenter. They went to the concession stand to grab something to eat.

Squatchsota pulsed with energy. The crowd had swelled to well over two hundred. Costumed attendees mingled with serious researchers, families, and the cryptid-curious. Some wore hairy suits, others had headbands with felt horns or carried plush Mothmen.

A man in a full Lizardman bodysuit walked by carrying nachos. Another waved a giant cardboard cutout of the Patterson-Gimlin frame.

"Only in America," Leon murmured.

Wayne nodded. "And blessed be for it."

At one booth, someone was selling t-shirts that read "I saw Bigfoot, no wait... that was just my mother-in-law." Another group of teens debated whether the Mothman or the Jersey Devil would win in a cage match.

Wayne stood beside Leon near one of the side pillars, munching on a soft pretzel. His coat was open, and his gray scarf hung loose. He nudged Leon with his elbow and grinned.

"Look at this lot," he said. "Stranger bunch than those chasing a wheel of cheese down Cooper's Hill."

Leon smirked. "Didn't you take part in it years ago?"

"Hey. I was a different person back then," Wayne chuckled.

Nearby, Brad and Zachariah joined them, each holding plates loaded from the indoor concession stand.

Brad lifted a spoonful of chili and nodded appreciatively.

"This is top notch," he said. "Nothing beats a hearty bowl in the winter."

Zachariah tore into a grilled panini. "I'm definitely not complaining," he agreed. "The bread is awesome."

Leon turned to Brad. "Tell me about those tours you run

in Tennessee," he said. "What's involved?"

Brad's eyes brightened. "I lead small groups under special permit into the Great Smoky Mountains National Park. We conduct ecological surveys, set up motion-activated trail cameras, document footprint casts and tree-break patterns, then hold night-time stakeouts with targeted call playback. Guests get hands-on field training, data-collection experience and a genuine chance to capture vocalizations under supervision."

Leon raised an eyebrow. "That sounds interesting. Ever had any success?"

Brad grinned. "We've cast about a dozen footprints. I've been escorted out more times than I can count. "Rocks get hurled into camp at night, and sometimes you can actually hear them moving amongst the tents."

Leon raised an eyebrow. "Ever felt threatened?"

Brad nodded. "Yeah. Those screams at midnight will wake the skeptic in you."

CHAPTER 16

luk's eye burned with anticipation as he stood just inside the treeline, muscles coiled beneath thick hair. His gaze followed ten others, Matto, and the rest of the warriors, as they slipped silently between the dark trunks. They ran ahead, shadows among shadows, moving with the certainty of hunters. Aluk wanted to see what lay beyond first. He stayed rooted, listening to the sound of their footfalls fading into silence as they crept toward the edge of the forest.

Aluk watched the lights of the town glow on the horizon, pale fire against night. Ahead of him the hairless ones walked among metal machines and bright windows, oblivious to the threat forming just beyond the trees.

His eye flicked to Matto for a moment. The youth stood at the front of the group, his expression fierce. Then Matto gave a low, confident grunt and sprinted forward. One by one, the other nine erupted from the treeline. Their bare feet struck the frozen ground in unison, cracking ice and rattling gravel. They became a dark wave pouring out of the forest onto the narrow road.

Aluk waited until he heard the first roar from their ranks, deep, resonating terror. Then he exhaled and stepped from the shadows, eye fixed on the scene before him. The hairless ones spun in panic as they charged through the parking lot.

CHAPTER 17

Leon, Wayne, Brad, and Zachariah finished their snacks, plates empty, as Darryl Delgado stood at the podium again announcing the lineup for tomorrow.

"At nine sharp we have a field workshop led by Brad Samples in the forest behind the center. At ten thirty we reconvene here for a panel on footprint analysis with Dr Simmons and Ranger Hayes. Lunch follows at noon in the main hall. At one fifteen Professor Elena Vance presents 'Sasquatch Behavior and Ecology.' Then at three we close the day out with a live Q&A featuring all our speakers. Be on time or you'll miss half the action."

He was interrupted when a young man burst through the entrance, eyes wide and trembling. "Bigfoot...are running across the road... they're angry... they're coming this way!" He backed off, voice cracking with terror.

People near him turned and laughed.

Someone said, "That's just Gary in his costume, you fool."

"I'm serious," the young man yelled.

A man wearing a leather jacket with *"Ask me anything.*

I'm a Bigfoot Expert" on the back strode to the front glass door. He raised his voice over the laughter. "Everyone stay calm, I'll handle this."

He opened the front glass door and stepped out. A heartbeat later a scream ripped across the lot. The Bigfoot Expert's head hurtled back through the doorway with such force that it smashed through the glass panels. It rolled across the floor and came to rest upside down amid a spray of blood.

Then all hell broke loose.

Deafening high-pitched screams and roars erupted from the parking lot. People covered their ears and backed away in panic as creatures surged forward smashing through the glass.

Wayne felt vibrations in his chest and glanced at Leon, who was staring at the faces of the enraged Sasquatch running into the foyer. "What the bloody hell?"

Leon stood motionless, unable to process what he was seeing. Were these real? Was this a prank? No, they looked too damn real. Too damn tall.

He snapped out of it and grabbed Wayne's arm. "Move!" They ran across the floor, shoving chairs aside, and dove under the nearest table as the horde descended.

Nearby, Jenny screamed for her father. Randy pulled her behind a separate table, the one he'd put boxes of stock on. They crouched beneath the tablecloth, bodies pressed close.

"What in the hell is going on?" Randy whispered, holding Jenny's hand tight as they both tried to stay hidden.

In the corner of the room, Zachariah ducked behind a banner and crouched behind a stack of empty boxes. He whispered to himself, "Stay low. Stay low."

One of the horde skidded to a halt in front of a life-size cardboard cutout of a Sasquatch, head cocked as it peered behind the standee. With a snarl it tore the flimsy panel to shreds, cardboard fluttering like snow, then sprinted on.

Screams ricocheted through the space. Vendors abandoned booths. Coffee and food spilled across the floor. Some ran for exits. Others ducked under tables. In the mass rush, people shoved past one another, trampling the fallen in frantic desperation. A folding display collapsed as two tried to crawl beneath it.

Wayne crawled closer to Leon beneath their table, keeping his head down. "I can't believe this!" Another Sasquatch roared as it smashed a nearby booth.

Leon peered out to check if the path was clear of glass and debris. When the nearest creature shifted its focus toward a booth at the center of the hall, Leon whispered, "We have to move." He took a quick look around and saw a sturdier table closer to the middle where it was less open.

They slipped out from under their table and crawled beneath the next one, then scrambled to the following table and ducked under it just as another Sasquatch tore into the pretzel stand, sending baskets of broken display pieces and salty twists scattering across the tile.

Nearby, Jenny pressed herself flat against the floor beneath her table, Randy shielding her with his body, trying to still her sobs.

A young man slipped on a discarded hot dog, hitting the floor hard. One of the beasts ran straight over him, crushing his body into the floor as blood and guts spilled out.

Another creature stormed a booth where a couple had been selling Sasquatch-themed cupcakes. The stand exploded under its weight. Frosting and blood mixed on the floor as it crushed one of them underfoot.

A woman stood in front of her booth, eyes wide, and body rigid. Before she could cry out, one of the beasts seized her by the hair, yanked her forward, and smashed her skull against a steel pillar. Crimson arcs spattered across the polished tile as bone fragments rattled against the metal. Her body went limp, spine arching in a grotesque curve, and slid to the floor in a pool of dark, congealing blood.

Another man pulled a pistol from under his coat and fired at one of the charging beasts. The shots rang out loud and rapid. The 9mm rounds hit the Sasquatch in the chest and shoulder. It staggered slightly, turned to look at him, and let out a low growl. The bullets did nothing but annoy it.

It charged. The man barely got a fourth shot before the Sasquatch bore down on him. Its massive shoulder slammed into his chest, crushing him against a display table, his gun falling to the floor. Ribs snapped like brittle sticks. A geyser of blood erupted from his mouth and nose as his chest caved inward. Limbs went limp, and his lifeless body slid off the table, leaving a dark stain that spread across shattered merchandise.

Lyneve, crawled from behind a tipped bench and reached for the man's gun. Her hands shook as she gripped it and aimed at the back of the creature's head. She fired. Once, twice, then rapid-fire until the chamber clicked dry. Her shots hit true. The Sasquatch reeled forward and smashed face first into a folding plastic table, its legs buckling under the impact. It tumbled off the broken table onto the floor, twitching violently before falling still.

More screams filled the hall.

Leon lay flat beneath the table and spotted an older man looking dazed against a tilted chair. He called softly, "Come here," beckoning him toward the space under the table. The man hesitated, eyes locked on the chaos. Before Leon could reach out his hand, a ten-foot Sasquatch lumbered past, elbowing the man in the side of the face. He went flying, crashing into the wall with a sickening thud.

Leon's stomach churned at the brutality. He lowered his head to the floor, placing his cheek against the cold floor, mind reeling in disbelief.

At that moment Wayne watched two Sasquatch seize a tall, lean man in a "SQUATCH HAPPENS" t-shirt. They snapped at each other over his body, snarling in low, guttural tones. The man's raw, gurgling screams tore through the hall as they wrenched at his arms and legs in a grotesque tug of war. Wet, sickening cracks marked each break, arterial spurts of blood and clumps of tissue showering the floor. At the final snap his scream choked off, and the creatures discarded his shredded remains like refuse. One then vaulted over overturned chairs and gave chase to another attendee fleeing toward the restrooms.

A man in a Goatman suit had tried hiding behind a nearby vending machine. A Sasquatch grabbed him by the neck, bit into his shoulder, then paused. Blood sprayed from its mouth. It spit, made a face of disgust, then hurled the man headfirst into the metal support beam.

Leon swallowed hard. I guess they didn't like the taste of goat, he thought, and immediately scolded himself for the dark humor racing through his mind.

Steven Bengle, ran onto the stage, raised both hands and shouted into a microphone that had already shorted out. "Everyone just stay calm, they are just scared, they're our friends!" Before he could finish, a Sasquatch vaulted up onto the platform. It seized Bengle around the legs and swung him through the windows behind the podium. Panes of glass exploded outward, lacerating his clothing and skin as his body crashed against the frame. He dangled halfway through the shattered opening before slumping to the floor in a puddle of blood.

Jenny whimpered beneath her table as debris flew overhead. Randy held her close, whispering, "Stay down, stay down."

Nearby, Zachariah crouched behind the boxes, listening to the chaos in the hall. He glanced at an overturned table for cover, and decided against it.

He watched an older couple stumble through the jammed floor, limping toward an exit. "This way!" he called cautiously, gesturing for them to follow. They ducked past him, leaving Zachariah alone in the gloom.

The cold air and snow rushed through the broken windows. A Sasquatch's roar shook the rafters. Zachariah buried his head, every muscle tensed, waiting for the moment it might find him.

At a long table near the center, Wayne and Leon stayed perfectly still, watching the legs of their table shake as creatures smashed booths. Jenny and Randy sat behind a smaller round table, close together, breathing as quietly as they could. Jenny was trembling, her arms tight around herself, trying to stay small. The floor around them was slick with spilled coffee, blood, and human remains, footprints trailing toward the darkened corridors beyond the main hall.

At the concession stands, more screams rose as attendees tried to escape. A woman tried to hide beneath the chili stall when a Sasquatch seized her legs, dragged her out and stomped down on her back. Life drained from her eyes in an instant.

Zachariah lifted his head just enough to glimpse his new friends, Wayne, Leon, Jenny, Randy and even Brad, all staying low beneath their tables. Then the floor shuddered once more as a Sasquatch burst through a side window, dark hair, and glass shards swirling like a sudden storm.

****

Aluk stalked down the hallway, senses attuned for any remaining hairless ones. He took in the scene with grim satisfaction: tables overturned like broken bones, displays splintered beyond repair, and dark pools of blood pooling around the lifeless bodies of the hairless ones.

Sparks flickered from crushed concession carts and banners lay torn across the floor. He felt the thrumming power of his clan behind him, each warrior a promise of vengeance.

It was time to push beyond these broken walls and hunt those who had fled into the night. With a final glance at the chaos, Aluk slipped out through the shattered doors, ready to find more hairless ones under the moonlit sky.

CHAPTER 18

Sergeant Ramirez eased the cruiser down a side street, headlights slicing through the falling snow, radio crackling with dispatch updates. His partner for the night, Officer Jenkins, rode shotgun, cracking sunflower seeds between his teeth and flicking the shells into an empty coffee cup between his legs. His eyes scanned the cars in front and the side mirror.

"You catch the Wild game last night?" Jenkins asked, tossing another seed into his mouth. "Overtime goal was nuts."

Ramirez nodded. "Saw the highlight. I still think they need a better second line."

Jenkins scoffed. "Nah, man, Hartman's been carrying more than his share lately."

Before Ramirez could answer, the radio crackled. "Unit 12, respond to Duluth Conference Center for reports of multiple 'Bigfoot' sightings and possible attacks."

Both officers exchanged a glance and burst out laughing.

"Bigfoot conference," Jenkins said, grinning. "Probably just people in costumes."

"Hopefully," Ramirez replied. "But you know we have to check it out."

Five minutes later, they turned onto a main road and both froze. Dozens of cars lay crashed into one another, crushed against snowbanks, some flipped onto their sides. Dark shapes darted between mangled vehicles, lumbering around like living nightmares. Twisted metal caught the light, and deep, echoing roars rolled through the air.

Ramirez slammed on the brakes and leaned forward. "What the fuck is going on here? I can't get the cruiser through those cars."

He tapped his radio. "Dispatch, Unit 12 on scene. Looks like a warzone. We're going to check it out. Send more units immediately."

"Copy that, Unit 12," dispatch replied. "Additional officers enroute."

Jenkins slid off the passenger seat and unhooked the shotgun from the ceiling rack while Ramirez grabbed the AR-15. They each reached into the console and side compartments—Ramirez grabbed an extra 5.56 magazine, Jenkins stuffed additional slugs into his vest pouches.

The sergeant gave a quick nod. "We'll go in on foot. Stay sharp."

Ramirez slung the rifle over his shoulder. Jenkins racked a shell into the chamber.

"Aim for the head or center mass. Watch for gaps in their hide," Ramirez said.

Jenkins shook his head, muttering, "We're really shooting Bigfoots… you gotta be kidding me."

Ramirez said nothing. He moved ahead, rifle gripped tight, eyes scanning the shadows.

They advanced down the road, stepping over broken glass and debris. Two hundred yards from the conference center entrance they paused behind a flipped SUV, breath steaming in the cold air. Two Sasquatches lurked near a pile of wreckage, deep growls rumbling through their chests as they tore into a man, their nails raking through flesh and fabric. Blood soaked the snow beneath him. He didn't move.

Jenkins ground his teeth as he stared into the street. "I can't fucking believe what I'm seeing, Ramirez. They ain't no bears. They're freakin' real."

Ramirez glanced at Jenkins, voice low and firm. "This is exactly the time to shoot first and ask questions later, Jenkins."

He pointed toward the closest pair. "Target those two," he whispered. "Aim for their heads."

"On three," Ramirez counted under his breath. "One… two… three."

BOOM! BOOM! BOOM!

Ramirez raised his AR-15, the patrol rifle tight against his shoulder, and aimed for the Sasquatch's face. But the creature shifted suddenly, darted to the side in a burst of motion. The shots struck its shoulder instead. Each 5.56 round thudded into thick hide. The creature staggered but stayed on its feet.

Jenkins fired two slugs from the shotgun, the blasts tearing through the air. The Sasquatch howled, stumbling backward into a minivan before slowly collapsing to the cold ground. Dark blood oozed from the wounds.

The second creature roared and charged Jenkins's

position.

Jenkins dove behind an SUV, firing twice more. The shots hit its hip and knocked it off balance. Ramirez stepped forward to cover Jenkins and fired two more rounds from his rifle at the creature's head. It collapsed onto the ice, twitching.

Ramirez advanced another ten yards to secure the fallen creature's path before another could flank him. Jenkins loaded more slugs into the shotgun. A third Sasquatch lurked near a shattered food truck, eyeing a frozen delivery man slumped inside. Jenkins raised the shotgun and fired. Two slugs slammed into the creature's lower spine. It dropped instantly, body twitching on the snow.

Suddenly, a cacophony of high-pitched screams erupted as more Sasquatches emerged from between wrecked vehicles. At least four others barreled out of the conference center, each one towering well over eight feet. Jenkins and Ramirez scrambled back behind the SUV, weapons at the ready.

One Sasquatch crashed through a shattered window of a nearby catering van, glass exploding like hail. A woman's panicked cry came from inside, and a second creature yanked her body from the wreckage. Ramirez raised the rifle once more. He fired three times, each bullet smashing into its ribcage. The beast roared, and Ramirez ended its life with another shot to its forehead.

He dropped the spent magazine into the snow and slammed a fresh one into the receiver with practiced hands.

Jenkins fired his shotgun at another charging creature. The bullets pounded its skull, but it stayed on its feet, roaring. Ramirez fired, hitting the beast in the cheek. It stumbled onto a snowbank, blood soaking the white.

They paused, rifle and shotgun aimed at the next approaching shape. More police cruisers rushed down the road, headlights bobbing through the snow. Officers poured out, pistols, rifles, and shotguns drawn, racing toward the chaos. Some skidded on ice, chasing shapes that vanished between wrecked cars.

A chorus of stunned voices carried in the cold.

"What the fuck?"

"Are those real?"

"Jesus Christ..."

Confusion turned to urgency as the echo of gunfire and savage roars rang out from the conference hall and the surrounding area, drawing even more creatures into the street.

Ramirez could see two new officers lobbing flashbangs toward a cluster of Sasquatches feasting on a hapless victim. One officer fired wildly into the air, trying to keep the creatures at bay. Ramirez yelled at him to shoot the damn things, not annoy them. Another officer moved to cover a wounded partner, who lay pinned under a fallen sign as a Sasquatch loomed above, ready to strike. Ramirez shot the beast in the head with his rifle. It collapsed on the wounded officer's leg with a wet thud.

Jenkins shouted, "Ramirez, behind you!"

A Sasquatch burst from the wreckage just yards away, hands flexed and teeth bared. Ramirez spun on his heel and fired twice, each round tearing into its thick chest. The beast staggered, let out a strangled roar, then pitched sideways into an abandoned sedan with a thunderous crash. Ramirez didn't hesitate. He stepped forward, braced his rifle, and squeezed the trigger again. The final bullet struck true in the creature's skull, and it collapsed in a heavy, echoing thud.

Jenkins turned and saw a Sasquatch grab a fallen officer by the torso and hurl him through the air. The body sailed past, slamming into two more officers and knocking them flat. One of them didn't get up.

Meanwhile, more officers marched down the street, forming a loose perimeter around the wreckage. Some were already engaged, blasting away with pistols, rifles and shotguns. A pair of Sasquatches ran toward a downed police cruiser. One officer dropped from the hood, clutching a leg wound. The beast roared with triumph, but Jenkins dropped it with two slugs from the shotgun. The other creature charged toward another squad car, ramming the door open. Officers inside fired wildly. Bullets ripped through the body, but it still tried to charge.

Ramirez and Jenkins advanced along the street, firing at any oversized shape. They ducked behind a battered delivery truck.

"This is crazy," Ramirez shouted over the howls.

"Stay focused," Jenkins shot back. "We need to clear a path for more units."

Sitrep crackled over the radio, new reports of Sasquatches spotted in the suburbs further north and south, attacking townsfolk in their homes and businesses. The ambulances were kept far from the chaotic scene.

One officer ran past them, shotgun slung across his shoulder, shouting for medical personnel to help a wounded colleague. Another emerged from behind a row of patrol cars, face ashen, firing his pistol at a Sasquatch tearing into a civilian. Ramirez fired five quick rounds from his rifle. The creature reeled, collapsing in the snow.

He dropped the spent magazine into the snow and slammed a fresh one into the receiver with shaky hands.

Jenkins seized the moment and sprinted toward a collapsed wall of crates where a man lay pinned beneath debris, just as a Sasquatch turned and began charging toward him.

Ramirez covered Jenkins as he slid between broken boards and grabbed the man by the arm, pulling him free. The Sasquatch roared. Ramirez leveled his rifle and fired twice, then dove out of the way. Jenkins joined him, firing both barrels from the shotgun point-blank. The beast thudded to the frozen ground.

Jenkins popped open the shotgun and slid in more slugs, hands working fast and dirty.

More cruisers lined the road, officers firing from the safety of their doors. Bright muzzle flashes lit up the falling snow. Sasquatches bounded between wreckage, still relentless. One sprinted at a mounted patrol unit, flipping it onto its side. Two officers inside leaped clear and emptied their pistols into its flank, the rounds skittering off uselessly.

The beast responded by seizing both men by their necks, crushing them together with bone-shaking force, then hurling them through the shattered windshield. It roared in triumph and padded onward through the carnage.

Jenkins shouted, "We need to push them back into the woods!"

Ramirez nodded, reloading his rifle as he surveyed the lot. "On my count. One… two… three!"

They fired in unison with their weapons, rounds tearing into the closest three beasts. Two collapsed instantly; the third staggered, roar fading into a gurgle before it crumpled.

Other officers advanced with their carbines blazing.

Each Sasquatch that tried to break cover was met with a wall of lead. Some dropped where they stood, others staggered under the hail of bullets, roaring in agony before finally falling.

Still, more emerged from storefronts, behind hulking wrecks, and from dark alleyways, eyes glowing in the streetlights. An officer tried a point-blank pistol shot, the round glancing harmlessly off thick hair as the creature turned and charged on. The chaos never relented.

Ramirez swept the perimeter with his rifle. "We can't

keep this up. We don't have the ammunition."

Jenkins wiped his forehead, snowflakes melting into the blood smeared across his face. "We need more powerful weapons with immediate stopping power."

Ramirez yelled to approaching officers. "Get whatever you have. Assault rifles, shotguns, everything that can give us stopping power."

Jenkins turned to Ramirez, his voice on edge. "We're losing ground."

Ramirez raised his rifle. "Hold tight. We can't let them break through."

He'd burned through three magazines already. Another clicked into place as he scanned the street.

A new squad of officers arrived, running past overturned squad cars, bodies and debris. One yelled, "We've got snipers on the roof!"

Ramirez nodded. "Good. Keep their heads down. We'll clear the parking lot."

They advanced together, firing at any movement. A Sasquatch lunged at Jenkins from behind a stalled van. Jenkins twisted, raising his shotgun and fired two slugs into its face. The creature collapsed into a heap of dark hair and sharp teeth.

Ramirez spotted a young officer struggling to reload, rifle clattering to the snow. He dashed toward him, sliding the weapon into the officer's hands.

"Here," Ramirez said. "Keep firing."

The young officer nodded, hands shaking as he fired repeatedly at advancing shapes.

Ramirez kept moving, clearing a narrow path toward the front of the lot. Blood and broken glass crunched underfoot. An officer to his left was swarmed by three creatures. He fired six quick rounds, two hitting center mass, but the creatures kept coming. Ramirez turned and saw Jenkins running toward him, shotgun empty, pistol raised. He fired at the nearest shape, hitting it in the neck. It acted like it had been stung by a pesky bee and kept running.

Jenkins grabbed a shotgun from a fallen officer. "We need to hold this spot," he said, voice raw.

Ramirez nodded. "Keep them in the lot, no letting them escape into the street."

The two men spread out, backing behind cars, firing from cover. More cruisers and sheriff's units parked in the distance, deputies, and state patrol officers pouring out alongside local FBI agents. They converged on the edges of the lot, shouting orders and trying to organize a final push.

CHAPTER 19

Michael crouched at the bottom of the basement stairs, rifle resting against his shoulder. Adam clutched his younger siblings to his chest, each soft sigh, and tremor echoing through the stairwell. The dog sat between them, shaking and whining so quietly that Michael wondered if he'd even heard it.

From upstairs came a rapid series of high-pitched chatter and deep grunts. Metal scraped against wood as something large collided with furniture. A cabinet fell, its pieces crashing to the floor above. Michael's eyes stayed fixed on the closed basement door, willing it not to open.

Footsteps rumbled over the hall stairs that led to the bedrooms, getting closer. The boards creaked as weight moved down the hallway toward their rooms. Michael's breath caught. He forced himself to draw air in tiny sips, sweat stinging his eyes.

A child's whimper rose in pitch, then the dog's whine cut sharp. Michael gripped the rifle with gloved fingers, every finger pressing into cold metal. He imagined the creature's shape, towering, dark hair slicked with snow, looming at the top of those stairs.

The footsteps halted. Silence spread, thick and suffocating. Michael felt his hands tremble a little. A crash came from the neighbor's house, a door ripping from its hinges or furniture smashing.

Without warning, the creature charged down Michael's hall stairs, each step a hammer blow. Its wet breath rattled the hallway. Michael's finger hovered over the trigger. He dared not exhale.

The Sasquatch ran straight through the front door, shattering wood and glass as they charged toward the screams from next door.

Michael sank against the wall, rifle still in hand. Adam held his siblings tighter, eyes wide as he peered up at his father. The dog stood, head low, ears pressed back. Michael pressed a palm to his damp forehead. No more noise followed.

He let his breath settle into a steady rhythm. The

basement door stood between them and whatever had roamed upstairs.

Michael hoped they would not be back, but he worried about the couple next door.

CHAPTER 20

Mara Gibbons hunched over her laptop in the back of the news van, the glow from the screen flickering across her face. They were close now. Too close to turn around.

She zipped her coat halfway, heart pounding beneath layers of fleece. This was it. The story. The one that would put her name in every headline and search bar. If even a second of footage came through with a real Sasquatch in frame, she would never again be handed puff pieces about mayoral bake-offs or pet parades.

Bryce, her cameraman, drove in silence. The windshield wipers struggled to push aside the thin sleet that streaked across the glass. Outside, the streets were chaos. Abandoned vehicles, flickering lights, shattered storefronts. Snow layered it all in a clean white skin that only made the destruction stand out more.

Mara glanced at her phone. No signal. Just a red "X." She opened the side window a crack. A low howl drifted in from somewhere to the east, followed by distant gunfire. She shut it quickly.

"We should set up soon," she said, breaking the silence.

"We don't want to be late to our own exclusive."

Bryce didn't look back. "Yeah, well, exclusive means jack if we get stomped into soup."

Mara checked her equipment again. Battery packs full. Backup drives ready. Mics synced. She slapped a hand to the wall of the van. "Take the next left. There's a ridge overlooking the north side. Sound carries up from there."

They turned, the van crunching over glass and debris, weaving around what had once been a billboard truck now wrapped around a utility pole. At the top of the slope, Bryce found a level spot and parked.

"You sure about this?" he asked.

She looked up from the laptop. "We'll be quick. Shoot ten minutes, tops. Then we're gone."

They sat there in silence for a moment, the van's engine ticking in the cold. Mara reached out and shut it off.

Bryce eased the van into park and climbed into the back, beginning to unpack equipment. The camera came out first, followed by the tripod, then a shoulder rig. He worked in silence, focused, efficient.

Mara smoothed her hair and dabbed at her cheeks with powder. She checked her reflection, lips tight, eyes fixed. Her hands shook slightly, but she forced her features calm.

"I'll go on mic," she said. "Keep wide to start. If we catch something, you zoom in."

Bryce slid the camera case open and inserted a fresh SD card. The sound of the latch clicking shut felt loud in the quiet van. He adjusted the rig, turned on the power pack, and checked the settings.

Outside, the wind shifted. There was a low, distant sound. Not a vehicle. Not a siren.

A roar.

It vibrated through the air like a rolling tremor, long and deep. Bryce froze, one hand still on the tripod.

"You hear that?" Mara asked. She didn't look up from her mirror.

"Yeah," he said quietly.

Another roar followed, this one closer. Then came the sound of something moving. It wasn't running, but it was heavy. Snow compressed beneath it, and something scraped the pavement.

They both paused.

Bryce set the tripod down slowly and reached for the side curtain. He didn't open it. He just listened.

A sudden impact struck the driver's side of the van. Metal screamed. The whole vehicle tilted on two wheels before crashing back down.

Mara screamed, makeup mirror clattering to the floor.

Mara stared at the warped ceiling, blinking fast as if trying to keep control.

Bryce pushed himself up slowly from the tangle of cords and gear, blood sliding down the side of his face. His hands shook as he reached for the overturned camera rig, then let it go, eyes wide. "Was that a Bigfoot?" he said, voice thin and rising.

"How the hell would I know?" Mara snapped, rubbing her elbow where it had slammed into the wall.

Bryce scrambled toward the back, leaning on shelving

for support. "We shouldn't have come here. This is insane.

You said we just needed a shot from the street. I didn't sign up for this."

"You didn't sign up for anything except holding a camera and driving," she said, shoving a cord off her boot. "Now do your job."

"The gear's trashed," he said, but she ignored him.

Mara crawled toward the front, wiping a smear of blood from her sleeve. She reached across the dash, pulled her phone from her coat pocket, and opened the camera app.

With a grunt, she pushed the button to lower the passenger window just enough and slid her phone outside, tilting it to get a clear shot of the road below. The record icon blinked red on the screen.

Then something hit the van.

The passenger window exploded inward in a spray of glass. A massive hand burst through the opening and grabbed her around the chest and neck, yanking her forward with terrifying force.

She let out a blood-curdling scream.

Then she was gone.

Bryce didn't make a sound. He stayed frozen, watching the empty space where she had just been.

He heard it all.

A horrible wet crunch.

A ripping noise.

Silence.

Then something spat.

The phone clattered onto the door sill, screen still glowing.

Inside the van, Bryce backed away from the window, crawling on hands and knees through the mess. His mouth trembled as he whispered nonsense to himself, the words breaking apart before they ever formed.

He stayed inside, knees tucked under him, arms over his head.

Outside, the van rocked.

The frame shifted.

He then felt the van being pushed.

Snow and ice gave way as the van began sliding, first

slow, then faster. It picked up speed and spun sideways before hitting the slope. The world rolled, once, twice. Gear smashed against the walls. A case split open. Lights and batteries spilled everywhere.

On the second roll, Bryce's head struck the metal base of the bench seat. His vision flared white, then went dark.

He came to with a jolt as the van slammed into something solid. A tree.

Silence followed.

Bryce lay half-sprawled among the wreckage, blood trickling from a fresh cut along his hairline. His thoughts swam, sluggish and cracked. A sharp ache pulsed behind his eyes as he grimaced and touched his forehead. He could feel pain elsewhere too, deep and throbbing along his ribs and legs, but he didn't dare shift. He had no idea how long he'd been unconscious, only that it was quiet now.

He stayed still.

He waited in the silence, surrounded by broken equipment and cold air, listening for footsteps he prayed would never come.

CHAPTER 21

The world under the conference table was a symphony of muffled terror. The frantic roars of the creatures, the screams of the dying, and the distant thud of heavy impacts vibrated through the floor. From somewhere outside, the crack of gunfire echoed through the walls, sporadic and sharp. They couldn't tell the direction, only that it was close.

Leon, usually composed, had a sheen of sweat on his brow, his spectacles slightly askew. Beside him, Wayne, despite his aching joints, moved with surprising stealth, peering through the gap between the tablecloth and the floor.

A truck had smashed through the front entrance earlier, now sitting half-embedded in the wall with smoke curling from its engine. Flames flickered across the mangled doorway, making escape that way impossible. Wayne had to stifle a cough as the acrid smoke started drifting beneath the tables and stinging his throat.

"Bloody hell," Wayne whispered, his voice shaky with fear. He subtly nudged Leon, angling his head towards the far wall. Tucked against it, partially obscured by a fallen banner, was young Zachariah. His eyes, wide with fear, met Wayne's. Wayne put a finger to his lips, a silent command for absolute stillness. Zachariah nodded, lowering himself further into the shadow.

Wayne shifted his gaze, scanning the devastation. A few tables over, beneath what remained of their booth, he spotted Randy and his daughter Jenny. They were pressed close together, barely visible under a cascade of shredded fabric and splintered wood. Randy's face was pale and rigid, his arm wrapped protectively around Jenny, who stared at the chaos with wide, unblinking eyes. Wayne caught Randy's gaze across the wreckage and gave a small, urgent nod, a silent plea to stay absolutely still. Randy responded with the faintest tilt of his head.

Then Wayne saw Brad crouched under a table opposite him. He raised a hand slowly, signaling without a word.

He slowly turned his attention back to the carnage. One colossal Sasquatch, its hair a dark, tangled mass, was tearing through the wreckage of booths and overturned tables.

Wayne didn't see any other Sasquatch and hoped they'd taken off or gone deeper into the building. This one moved with a terrifying blend of curiosity and destructive intent, a hunter methodically sniffing out prey. Its eyes gleamed with chilling intelligence as it paused at a pile of shredded merchandise, then casually flipped over a display stand that had once held commemorative Squatchsota mugs. The crash echoed through the relative silence of their hiding spot.

"He's looking for more," Leon mumbled, his Dutch accent barely audible, his voice tight.

"Aye, and he's getting closer," Wayne replied, his gaze fixed on the shifting hair of the beast, a raw edge to his tone. "We can't stay put. Not much longer, anyway."

Leon swallowed hard, his throat dry. "Where would we go? Out there?" He gestured vaguely to the open space beyond their flimsy cloth barrier, where debris created a jagged obstacle course.

"Better than waiting for him to lift this tablecloth like it's a tea cozy," Wayne countered, his voice a strained whisper. "We have to move. Now. Before he's right on top of us."

"And the others?" Leon asked, his gaze flitting from Zachariah to Randy and Jenny's hiding place, and finally to Brad.

Wayne nodded. "We take them with us. There's strength in numbers, even if it's just a few more limbs for them to chase." The grim humor was forced, but Leon understood the sentiment.

A plan, desperate and fragile, began to form. They would make a dash for the back exit, hoping the chaos there had thinned and offered a slim chance of escape. Wayne signaled Zachariah again, this time a series of quick, deliberate motions. He pointed to the exit, then to himself and Leon, then back to Zachariah, finally holding up three fingers. Zachariah, a quick study, seemed to grasp their intent. His youthful face hardened with grim determination. Wayne then carefully extended his hand, pointing to Randy and Jenny, then to the exit, repeating the three fingers. Randy, his eyes fixed on Wayne's movements, nodded slowly, pulling Jenny closer. He repeated the signals to Brad who nodded slowly.

Wayne held up his hand, three fingers extended. He slowly bent one down. Two.

Just as his finger began to curl for the final count, they heard something clattering from behind a crushed information booth. A man emerged coughing, his clothes torn, his hair disheveled. He scrambled over a heap of chairs, eyes wide with manic terror, and sprinted for the hallway leading to the restrooms.

Wayne and Leon froze, their eyes fixed on the man. Time seemed to warp, stretching taut as they watched him go. The Sasquatch, its back to him, swiveled its enormous head at the sound. It let out a deafening roar, a sound that ripped through and bounced against each of their ribs and launched itself forward.

The pursuit was shockingly fast, a blur of hair and muscle. The Sasquatch crashed through the remaining tables, scattering debris like confetti, as it gave chase. The man, screaming frantically now, disappeared down a long corridor, the Sasquatch thundering after him, its roars growing more distant with each heavy stride. A final, desperate shriek cut short by a sickening thud. Then, the muffled, wet thudding of heavy impacts began to reverberate faintly from down the corridor, a gruesome rhythm. This was their window.

Wayne's voice, a raw, strained whisper, cut through the sudden, horrifying quiet. "Now! Go, go, go!" Leon scrambled from under the table, pulling Jenny from her hiding spot. Randy, nervous but determined, pushed Zachariah ahead of him, then followed, shielding Jenny with his body. Brad was up last and followed them as they moved in a desperate, low crouch, weaving through the maze of overturned furniture and mangled bodies.

Their focus was absolute on the distant glow of the back

exit sign, a beacon of improbable hope. The floor was slick with something they did not want to identify. Footfalls echoed their hasty retreat, surprisingly loud in the momentary vacuum of the hall. The air grew colder as they neared the door. Smoke from the truck crash still clung to the air, mingling with the stench of blood.

When they reached it, Wayne grabbed the handle and shoved the door open, letting the cold wind slap across his face. The night beyond was dark and dangerous, but it was better than staying.

CHAPTER 22

Gunfire echoed off shattered walls. Smoke and snow blurred the air, and the street was slick with blood. Bodies, both human and Sasquatch, lay scattered across the lot outside the Duluth Conference Center.

Sergeant Ramirez scanned for movement, chest heaving, rifle nearly empty.

A figure emerged from the haze, steady and purposeful.

"Sheriff Chang," the man called out, flashing a badge streaked with blood. "What's the situation?"

Ramirez lowered his weapon just long enough to answer. "We're almost out of ammo. We need heavier firepower, and fast. We haven't even had a chance to sweep the conference center for survivors."

The sheriff wiped snow from his brow. "I saw one that must have been at least twelve feet tall. Civilians are firing back from their homes with whatever they have. Thankfully, a substantial number of people in Minnesota are gun owners."

Ramirez's eyes widened. "Holy shit. That tall?"

Chang nodded. "And the good news is every agency is plugged into a unified Incident Command System. We've got air support on call, medevac crews standing by, and a coordinated public messaging network pushing alerts right now."

Ramirez stared into the chaos of twisted metal and torn bodies. "How the heck is any of this happening?"

Chang sighed, shouldering his rifle. "Lord if I know. Let's keep moving."

A man in a dark green uniform pushed pass some deputies and hurried over. He wore a Department of Natural Resources badge on his chest. "Where can I help?" he asked.

Ramirez glanced at the badge and raised an eyebrow. "You knew these things were real, didn't you?"

The DNR officer said nothing, his gaze level.

Ramirez shook his head. "Thought as much."

It's been in the news lately," the DNR man offered quietly. Ramirez snorted. "Like anyone trusts what the media shows. Just stick with us. If you see something big moving, aim for the head."

Up ahead, a small group of Sasquatches clambered over a pile of wreckage, eyes fixed on the humans ahead. Ramirez raised his rifle and fired two rounds at the lead figure's head. It recoiled, bouncing off a dented door, then crumpled to the ice.

Jenkins kept his shotgun aimed at the rest. "Two more down, three left in that group."

Ramirez swallowed, voice low. "We can do this."

They forced their way forward, edging closer to the lot's entrance with each volley. Snow wrapped around their boots, slurring the trail of footprints. Each flash of a muzzle revealed another shape retreating into the shadows.

Suddenly, a Sasquatch hurtled out from behind a ruined truck on all fours, its amber eyes blazing with fury. Ramirez dove aside and unleashed four rapid rifle shots while Jenkins hammered the trigger of his shotgun. The creature skidded across the ice bank, tumbled into a series of clumsy flips, then collapsed into the snow, utterly still.

Jenkins loaded a few more slugs into the shotgun, eyes scanning the lot. "Looks like we've driven them back."

Ramirez exhaled, slowly lowering his pistol. "For now. But I doubt they're gone for good."

He looked out over a battlefield of broken bodies and scattered gear. Twisted limbs jutted from beneath crushed vehicles. Blood streaked the ice in long, dark trails. Spent shell casings glinted among the debris as officers moved through the wreckage, dragging the wounded to safety.

Ramirez scanned the law enforcement officers around him, at least fifteen of them, fanning out in a loose perimeter.

Swirling snow muffled the distant howls.

Ahead, the conference center doors lay shattered, the foyer blocked by a truck that had crashed through the front wall. Ramirez cursed under his breath. "We're gonna have to find a way past that truck or look for another way inside."

Jenkins leveled his shotgun at the flickering lights beyond the wreckage.

Jenkins spoke low, "Let's try it."

They advanced across the snowy ground toward the broken doors of the center, weapons raised and breaths misting in the cold air, ready for whatever lay inside.

CHAPTER 23

It had been a week since Echo Black stormed the sanctuary to extract Rob, who had been kidnapped and held deep within Aluk's territory. The mission had taken a brutal toll. Four members of the team were injured. Many of Aluk's clan were killed. Since then, the team had remained in Duluth while the wounded recovered in hospital. The rest ran drills, reviewed footage, and waited, eager to get back into the field. Ideally somewhere warmer.

Now they were at Duluth International Airport, parked beside a private jet on the far ramp. The SUV idled as they offloaded gear in the freezing wind, readying for departure to San Antonio.

Jonah Briggs' secure phone buzzed in his jacket. He stepped away from the group to take the call.

"Briggs," came the clipped voice on the other end.

"Eastern Duluth is overrun. Sasquatch in large numbers. Law enforcement is outmatched. We need Echo Black to deploy now."

Jonah kept his voice level. "Do we go full team?"

"Negative. You're down four already. Take two. No further casualties, Briggs. That's an order."

"Copy that," he said, ending the call.

He returned to the SUV. The others had paused, watching him. Jonah never shouted. He didn't have to. His presence was enough.

"Sasquatch have taken over East Duluth. Command needs only three of us on this one," he announced. "Everyone else heads to Texas. We'll see you in San Antonio."

Diesel opened his mouth. Breaker shifted forward. Wildcat gave a sharp shake of her head. Rook bristled. Valkyrie glanced toward Whisper.

Jonah raised a hand. "Orders are orders."

His gaze settled on Havoc and Reaper. "You two. Gear up. Five minutes."

Darius Havoc Jefferson grinned and opened his gear bag. He pulled free the Knight's Armament LAMG and slung it over one shoulder. Grenade launcher next, the M320 sliding into place with practiced ease. He clipped extra belts across his chest and checked each mag by feel.

Miguel Reaper Cortez said nothing. He adjusted the scope on his M110 SASS and slung it to his back. His sidearm, a Glock 20, was already secured. Everything he did was efficient and methodical. Cold.

Jonah strapped on his SCAR-H and checked the FNX-45 at his hip. He gave a short nod.

"Comms on channel two," he said. "We're linking up with local units on the east side."

Havoc tapped his headset. "Locked in."

Reaper gave a nod and started walking.

The rest of the team stood silently at the base of the plane's stairs, watching them go. None of them liked being left behind, but they understood.

Jonah turned toward the SUV. "Let's move."

CHAPTER 24

The burst from the back exit was less a triumphant escape and more a violent expulsion into a new, terrifying reality. The snowy chaos of the building's back lot was a visceral assault. The air, already thick with the metallic tang of blood and the acrid bite of smoke, was now laced with the sharp chill of fresh snow.

The screams in the conference hall, though slightly muted, were replaced by a closer, more immediate symphony of destruction: the crunch of metal, the splintering of glass, and the guttural bellows of Sasquatch in the midst of their rampage.

Leon stumbled, his spectacles immediately fogging in the cold air, his refined senses overwhelmed. Wayne, despite his arthritis, moved with a surprising burst of speed, pulling Jenny forward. Brad instinctively took the lead, his voice firm and decisive. "Stick together and keep moving. We can't stop here." Randy, Jenny's father, a man whose hands usually carved wood with delicate precision, now gripped Zachariah's shoulder with desperate strength, urging the boy ahead.

"Stay low. Keep close," Brad ordered, guiding them through the debris-strewn back lot. Dumpsters lay overturned, trash and shattered crates littering their path. Every shadow felt alive, every twisted metal container a possible hiding spot for whatever still lurked.

At the rear boundary of the lot, they came to a chain-link fence torn open at the bottom. Brad pointed to the gap. "Crawl through, quick."

They dropped to the snow-covered ground, dragging themselves under the jagged fence edge. Jenny and Leon went first, their coats catching briefly before scrambling clear. Wayne groaned softly as his joints protested, forcing himself under with a grunt. Randy guided Zachariah through and then crawled in behind him, glancing back the whole time.

Brad was the last to go, scanning behind them. As he rose to his feet on the other side, an ear splitting, primal roar exploded from somewhere close in the lot they'd just left. The fence behind them rattled, and Brad's heart skipped a beat. "Move. Now," he said sharply.

Behind the conference center, a row of small businesses stretched out next to each other. A pizza joint. A shuttered hair salon. A convenience store with its front window smashed open. Shards of glass glittered in the snow. The storefronts looked empty, but who knew if another monster was hiding inside. They hurried past in the heavy silence, their shoes sliding on the icy slush.

They rounded a corner behind the last row of small businesses, the freezing air clouding their breath, when Brad slowed, his arm snapping out to halt the others.

"There," he said, pointing.

A large white SUV sat parked just ahead, engine still running. Exhaust spilled into the cold night air, and the headlights cast long beams across the road. The windows were up, the front doors wide open. No one was inside.

Brad jogged to it, eyes on the shadows. "Everyone in. Now."

By habit, Leon went straight to the driver's seat. A dead body lay crushed on the ground outside the door, ribs caved in, one arm twisted beneath it. He stepped over it, nearly gagging. Behind him, Randy shielded Jenny's face and hurried her past.

Leon adjusted his glasses as he climbed behind the wheel. Wayne slid into the passenger seat, grunting with effort. Jenny jumped in next, followed quickly by Brad and Randy in the back seat. Zachariah didn't hesitate. He climbed into the trunk space, pulling the hatch shut behind him.

"Drive," Brad snapped.

Leon's hands fumbled at the gear stick. "I'm trying," he said, voice shaking.

The SUV lurched forward.

Wayne pointed out the windshield. "You're on the wrong side of the road."

Randy didn't even glance up. "Probably doesn't matter right now."

The tires lost traction for a moment as they careened around a corner into a quiet residential street. Houses loomed ahead, dark and silent behind thin curtains of falling snow.

Then, from the left, a shape exploded out of the gloom.

A Sasquatch, smaller than the others but still massive, maybe six feet tall, sprinted directly into their path.

"Oh shit," Brad said, just before impact.

The SUV slammed into the creature head-on. The sound was sickening. The Sasquatch hit the hood, then the windshield, and smashed clean through it. Its head snapped backward as its body slammed into the center console and kept going. Instinctively, everyone leaned away from the hurtling mass, but in the middle seat, Brad was directly in its path. The back window shattered as the Sasquatch's skull burst through. Shards of glass rained down.

For a moment, everything was still.

The Sasquatch lay sprawled across the seats, massive and unmoving. Its feet were draped over the dashboard, knees bent at odd angles. The torso sagged heavily across the back seat area, pinning Brad beneath it. One arm dangled over Jenny's lap, the other hung limp against Randy's leg. Its head jutted through the rear window, hair dirty, jaw slack. Broken glass framed its skull like jagged ice.

Blood was everywhere. It soaked the seats, smeared across the ceiling, and pooled in the grooves of the upholstery.

It was still breathing. Shallow and wet. A faint gurgle from somewhere deep in its chest.

Jenny screamed, frozen in place.

The Sasquatch's bloody hand rested in her lap.

Zachariah's voice came from the back. "I need help. I'm stuck. It's on me."

Randy scrambled out of the vehicle the moment he realized Brad wasn't moving. Brad's head had fallen into his lap, lifeless. Glass clung to his hair.

They spilled out into the freezing street.

Leon turned toward the SUV. "Where's Brad?"

Randy leaned against the side of the car, trying to catch his breath. Blood soaked the front of his jacket and pooled in his lap, smeared from where Brad's head had rested. He didn't look up. "He's still in there."

Leon started to move toward the rear passenger door, but Randy reached out and placed a hand on his chest.

"Don't look," he said.

Leon froze. The message was clear.

Zachariah climbed out of the trunk with Wayne's help. He stood shaking, lips pressed tight, blood matting one sleeve. He sniffed once and winced. "It stinks. Like sewage and rot."

Jenny looked down at herself, finally registering the blood smeared across her sleeves and jeans. "Oh my God," she said, voice rising. "It's all over me. I can't... I can't breathe." She pulled at her jacket, frantic, her hands trembling.

Randy pulled her close and held her. "It's okay," he whispered, stroking her back. "You're okay. You're safe."

She buried her face against him, crying, while the others stood silent.

Zachariah looked up the street, his voice quieter now. "Uh... guys. Up there. More of them."

Two Sasquatch were pounding on a front door, slamming their shoulders into it with bone-jarring force. The frame cracked under the weight of each hit.

Wayne scanned the street and spotted a house with its door already open. "In there. Now."

Leon hesitated. "What if one of them is already inside?"

Wayne didn't slow. "We're shit outta luck then. We can't stay out here."

As they ran, Leon shouted, "What about Brad?"

Randy's voice came hard and final. "There's no time."

They ran, feet slipping slightly on the snow-covered pavement, breath ragged, hearts pounding, leaving the wrecked SUV and Brad behind.

They didn't dare look back. Muscles burning, lungs raw, they pushed on. The porch was only steps away. They rushed through the doorway and collapsed into the darkness, pulling the broken door shut behind them as best they could.

CHAPTER 25

Jonah Briggs gripped the wheel as the SUV crept down a snow-dusted suburban street lined with quiet houses and darkened storefronts. The sky above was flat and colorless. .

A fast-food place sat on the corner with all its windows shattered inward, glass scattered across the parking lot like frozen confetti. The neon sign above flickered once and died. No one was in sight. Not a pedestrian. Not a single car. Just the wind and drifts of snow moving through a place that had emptied far too fast.

In the back seat, Reaper stared out the side window, his rifle balanced across his knees. "Why are they out in the open?" he said quietly. "They've never done this before. Not like this."

Havoc was halfway through his second protein bar, chewing with gusto. He mumbled around a mouthful,

"Retaliation. We went into their home didn't we?"

Reaper gave him a sidelong look and shook his head. "You really can eat at a time like this?"

"Gotta fuel the machine," Havoc said, winking. "Can't crush skulls on an empty stomach."

"Besides, we've done that with other clans before," Reaper added quietly. "They never came out of the forest and attacked townsfolk on this scale."

Jonah remained silent, eyes fixed ahead, his grip steady on the wheel.

"Did they give you coordinates on where this is all going down?" Havoc asked, brushing crumbs off his vest.

Before Jonah could answer, a hulking shape tore across the road ahead. It moved on all fours, fast and low, a blur of dark hair and limbs. It disappeared into the side yard of a two-story house with its porch light still on.

"I think we are in the right place," Jonah said quietly.

"Yeah, that was no well-fed Rottweiler." Havoc said.

He pulled the SUV to the curb on the next block and killed the engine.

"Stay tight. Stay focused. We don't know how many there are or where they're holed up."

They exited the vehicle and moved fast, cutting behind a strip of small businesses. A sandwich shop had its front window smashed out, chairs and napkins strewn into the street. A laundromat stood dark and still. A pharmacy's shelves had been knocked over inside.

Havoc glanced through the shattered door. "Oh great. Just what we need. Sasquatch high on drugs."

The snow was falling harder now, beginning to soften the edges of destruction.

They passed between the buildings and crossed into a residential street. Mailboxes had been flattened. A tricycle lay overturned in a driveway. The wind was louder here, funneling between houses, but the rest of the world had gone quiet.

A sedan sat skewed across a lawn, its rear window spiderwebbed with cracks. Jonah raised a hand, signaling them to slow.

"Two o'clock," Reaper said.

Two Sasquatch charged out from behind a detached garage, barreling straight toward them. No hesitation. Just raw speed.

"Contact," Jonah said, voice clipped and calm.

Havoc braced and fired. The LAMG let out a rapid burst. A short line of rounds struck the lead Sasquatch, two to the thigh, one to the knee. The creature stumbled violently, crashing forward. Jonah followed with a single, clean shot to the head. The body went still before it hit the ground.

The second Sasquatch swung wide, arms low and eyes locked on Havoc. Reaper took two quick steps to the left, raised his rifle, and fired once. The round punched through the creature's skull just above the jawline. Its body folded instantly, dropping with a muffled thud into the snow beside a mailbox.

They held position for a beat, scanning for movement.

"Two down," Jonah said. "Let's keep moving."

They pushed on, weaving through a tangle of yards and alleys. Behind them, the faint sound of gunfire still echoed somewhere further south. They passed a corner restaurant with its door ripped off the hinges. Tables were overturned. One still had a plate of food on it, half-buried in snow.

As they came around the far side of the building, two men emerged from the shadows near the intersection. Both carried shotguns. They had sidearms holstered at their hips, gear that looked hastily scavenged. Their police-issued uniforms were dirty and torn, sweat soaking through their snow-dusted jackets.

One of the men stepped forward. "Sergeant Ramirez, Duluth PD," he said, his voice hoarse. He gestured to the man beside him. "This is Officer Jenkins."

Ramirez's eyes dropped to their rifles, widening slightly as he took in the gear.

"You military?" he asked.

"Something like that," Jonah replied. "You alright?"

Ramirez nodded, but it was slow and tired. "We just pulled back from the conference center. It's clear. The only things in there now are bodies. Ours and theirs."

Jonah looked them over. "You short on ammo?"

"Not anymore," Ramirez said. "We grabbed what we could off the fallen. Shotguns. A couple sidearms and some ammo from a cruiser. That's it."

Jonah nodded once. "You're welcome to follow with us."

Ramirez looked between the three of them, then gave a half-smile. "We will. You three look like you know what you're doing."

"Not our first rodeo," Havoc said, voice clear with a faint edge of pride.

Reaper said nothing, just adjusted his grip on the rifle and kept his eyes scanning the rooftops.

Jonah motioned forward. "Let's keep going."

They started walking again, boots crunching over ice and broken debris. As they passed a tipped-over mailbox and moved deeper into the residential sprawl, Ramirez suddenly slowed and turned toward Jonah.

"I need to ask," he said, voice tight. "My family lives about ten blocks from here. Phones are jammed. I've been trying to call them all night. Nothing's going through."

Jonah looked over at him. "How far?"

"Ten blocks, maybe eleven," Ramirez said. "Just past the high school."

Jonah glanced at Havoc and Reaper.

Havoc gave a nod.

Reaper simply said, "Let's move."

Jonah turned back to Ramirez. "We're heading that way

anyway."

Ramirez swallowed hard, then nodded. "Thanks."

They left the broken storefronts behind and moved on, deeper into the neighborhoods where porch lights flickered behind curtains and the wind carried distant echoes of things still moving in the dark.

CHAPTER 26

Isaiah adjusted the last row of canned energy drinks, the metal clinking as he slid them into a straight line. His headphones pulsed with the distorted shriek of a metal-punk fusion track, drums hammering, guitar lines screaming. He bobbed his head slightly in time with the music, lost in it.

The gas station was dead quiet. Not a car had pulled in for hours, which struck him as strange. Usually, he'd see a few locals swing through for smokes or a drink, maybe someone gassing up before a night drive. But tonight, nothing.

He paused with a can in his hand, blinking at the windows. The fluorescents inside cast a harsh glare on the glass, but beyond it, the road was deserted. Not even a racoon or passing car. Just stillness.

He shrugged and dropped the last can into place, then headed behind the counter. His insulated drink cup waited for him, half-filled with watered-down soda. He grabbed it, took a long pull, and let the cold hit his throat.

Then he noticed headlights in the distance.

He squinted and leaned toward the window, pulling off one headphone. The music still buzzed in one ear, but he wasn't listening.

A sedan tore down the hill, headlights bouncing as it swerved left and right. Something was on the roof. Sprawled flat on its stomach, a creature pounded at the roof with long arms, its fists denting the metal. The windshield was spiderwebbed with cracks, and through it, Isaiah saw the terrified face of a woman behind the wheel. Her mouth was open in a silent scream.

The car swerved again. It was coming straight for the pumps.

Isaiah's mouth opened, but no sound came out. The sedan clipped the curb, skidded, then slammed into the nearest fuel pump. A massive explosion tore through the station.

The fireball lifted the front of the building and sent Isaiah flying backward. He hit the floor hard, air knocked from his lungs. For a second, all he saw was flickering orange against the ceiling. Glass rained down. The power flickered and died.

He coughed and rolled to his side, ears ringing, limbs slow to respond. The air was thick with smoke. A reddish glow pulsed outside the shattered front windows where the pumps had been. The sedan was nothing more than a burning husk. The thing on the roof was laying on the ground, smoldering.

He staggered to his feet and stumbled to the counter, breathing hard. The music had cut off. Only faint crackling reached him now from outside.

Then movement. Another shape crossed the road.

This one walked upright.

Not a person.

"What the fuck", Isaiah mumbled out loud.

Larger. Heavier. Covered in coarse, matted auburn hair. It stalked out of the shadows, drawn by the blast. The light from the burning wreck cast its silhouette in grim relief. Its head swung side to side, nostrils flaring then its eyes locked onto Isaiah.

He ducked behind the counter, heart racing. He reached blindly for the baseball bat he kept near the register but couldn't find it. His fingers scraped across spilled receipts and his dropped drink.

A crunch of glass outside the front door.

He crawled low toward the back. Every instinct screamed to run, but his legs barely obeyed. As he reached the corridor that led to the restrooms, a deafening crack sounded as something pushed its way through the damaged front door.

Heavy footfalls entered the store.

Isaiah scrambled into the restroom and slammed the door behind him. The dull light above buzzed once, then flickered. He shoved himself into the corner farthest from the entrance, heart pounding so hard he thought it might burst.

The Sasquatch hit the restroom door once. The hinges popped. A second hit buckled the center. Isaiah whimpered without meaning to.

The third hit splintered it open.

The creature filled the doorway. Its eyes locked onto Isaiah, lips peeling back. It stepped inside, stooping to fit. It didn't roar. It didn't lunge. It just walked forward with absolute certainty.

Isaiah raised his hands. "Please," he gasped.

The creature grabbed him.

It lifted him with one hand, slammed him against the tiled wall, then brought him down hard onto the floor. Bones cracked. Isaiah screamed.

The Sasquatch dragged him by one leg, turned him upside down, and shoved his head into the toilet bowl. His legs kicked once, then stopped.

Blood dripped from the rim. The only sound was the wind through the broken windows and the sound of fading footsteps crunching over broken glass.

CHAPTER 27

Darkness filled the house, swallowing every trace of the snow-lit chaos outside. The front door hung loose from its hinges, leaning against the frame but offering a bit of cover. Their ragged breaths broke the silence. The air felt cold, edged with dust and a faint hint of gunpowder.

Wayne leaned against the doorway, drawing an unsteady breath. "Water," he croaked, voice rough. His throat burned; his mouth felt like sand. The need pressed on him more fiercely than fear.

Leon's glasses caught the dull light filtering through broken door as he scanned the entryway. "Stay still," he whispered, voice low but clear. "Listen."

They froze. Only the hiss of snow against glass and distant roars from the street reached them. No footsteps or snarls came from within. Yet the threat of something unseen in the shadows weighed on all of them.

Randy pulled Jenny close, arm firm against her shaking shoulder. She leaned her forehead into his chest. Zachariah crouched against the far wall, knees drawn up, eyes flicking between dark corners.

Wayne pushed off the frame, legs wobbly, but the need for water drove him forward. "I just need a sip," he said, wobbling down the hallway. Every step made the whole floor creak loudly in the quiet.

"Wait, Wayne," Leon whispered, but Wayne's foot hit another board and a low voice roared up from below.

"Who's there? Show yourself!"

The sudden shout sent panic through them. Randy yanked Jenny behind him. Wayne stumbled back, nearly losing his balance. Leon raised both hands in peace. "We're just looking to get off the street. We won't hurt anyone," he said, voice firm even in the darkness.

The man swung the flashlight across each of them, studying their faces. His gaze lingered on Jenny's trembling expression, then on Zachariah's alert stance, and finally on Randy's protective posture. His expression softened. He pushed the basement door open wider, revealing a small but secure refuge below.

"Michael," he said quietly. "Michael Hoffman. I shot one that came through here earlier." He gestured back toward the darkened path to the kitchen. "I've heard others come in since, but they left. We've been hiding down here. Me and my kids."

Leon nodded. "Thank you for not shooting. There are many of them out there."

"Tell me about it," Michael mumbled, stepping fully into the hallway. He was a solidly built man in a stained T-shirt and jeans, arms thick with muscle. His eyes, though tired, still held a fierce spark. "I am glad to see some people have made it through."

"We were lucky," Wayne said, eyes fixed on Michael's face. "Very lucky. Any chance of water? My throat's on fire."

Michael glanced at Wayne, noticing his cracked lips and strained expression. "Kitchen's that way," he said, swinging the flashlight to illuminate the path. "Don't trip on the dead Bigfoot."

Wayne sighed and moved carefully toward the kitchen. Leon turned back to Michael. "Could we hide in the basement with you and your kids?"

Michael looked at the group, then back at his children. His voice was steady. "Does anyone here know how to shoot a gun?"

With a resounding "yes," Zachariah and Randy stepped forward.

Michael nodded. "Go to the hall cabinet and grab a shotgun and some shells. Come on down, but you have to stay absolutely quiet and not get in the way."

Randy gave a faint nod. "Thanks. You'll have no trouble with us."

CHAPTER 28

The wind howled through the empty streets as Echo Black moved through Duluth's shattered neighborhoods. Broken signs and scattered debris littered the way forward. Every corner echoed with distant roars and the occasional scream. Up ahead, an Applebee's sat dark and abandoned. Posters hung torn on the front windows. The glass in the entry was cracked, and the interior was a mess of overturned chairs and shattered dishes.

Jonah slowed, eyes narrowing as he spotted movement inside. A hulking figure shifted near the kitchen pass-through.

He raised a fist. "Halt."

He turned to Ramirez. "Secure the front with Jenkins. Keep eyes on the street."

Ramirez nodded. "You got it. We'll hold it down."

Jonah looked to his team. "Havoc, cover the left. Reaper, take the fire escape across the street. Provide overwatch and keep low. I'll move through the center."

Havoc gave a grin, already moving. "Nothing like showing these bastards who's boss."

Reaper didn't respond, just slipped away silently, rifle tucked close. His boots barely made a sound as he vanished up the fire escape.

Each man moved into position.

As Jonah pushed through the shattered doors, the stench of the beasts mixed with the thick, iron scent of death. Bodies were everywhere, crushed and torn, some half-buried beneath broken tables. Blood coated the floor in wide, dark smears. The smell nearly overpowered him.

Inside, the lights flickered overhead. Tables were overturned. Menus and plates covered the floor. Broken wine glasses and shattered picture frames lay along the bar.

Jonah crouched near a booth, rifle raised. He peered through a gap in the service window. The hulking shape was still pacing near the kitchen. Its hair hung in greasy knots. Massive shoulders flexed with each step.

Havoc moved into position and raised his LAMG.

"Say cheese," he mumbled, then fired.

Two quick shots to the temple. The creature's head snapped back. Blood splashed across the prep counter. The beast staggered and crashed face first into a vat of oil, hot grease sloshing onto the floor.

From the hallway, another scream. A second Sasquatch, already wounded, barreled from the corridor near the bathrooms.

Jonah turned and fired. Two quick shots to the skull. The creature dropped in a heap of limbs and blood.

Havoc moved behind the counter, barrel still warm. Black blood streaked the flooring. The dining area was a wreck. Broken chairs. Spilled condiments. Not a single thing left intact.

"Clear," Havoc said. "Smells worse than my first barracks."

Jonah checked the corpses. Even dead, the creatures were massive. The only thing that stirred was a ceiling fan turning in lazy circles above them.

He turned back to Ramirez and Jenkins. They were still at

the entrance, eyes scanning the street.

"Move up. We're clearing the back."

Ramirez gave a low whistle. "You guys don't waste time."

Jenkins, younger and wide-eyed, followed close behind. "I've seen some stuff today, but that was something else."

They regrouped in a narrow hallway. The wind howled through a shattered window in the kitchen. The air reeked of grease, spilled alcohol, urine, and wet dog.

The first storage door stood cracked. Jonah shouldered it open. Inside, only broken boxes and fallen shelves.

The next room felt colder. A walk-in cooler sat at the back, its door hanging ajar.

Jonah raised his hand. "Ready."

He threw it open.

Inside, two Sasquatch stood at the far wall, hunched near fallen meat crates. Both turned, eyes glowing orange.

Jonah fired. Two rounds through its eye. The first creature dropped instantly.

The second roared and charged Havoc. It swung wide. Havoc dove to the side and fired a burst into its chest. Jonah stepped in and fired one clean shot into the back of its head. The beast spun, hit the shelving, and slid down in a heap.

Jonah held still. Listened.

"Clear," he said.

The blood from the fallen creatures soaked the floor. Their heat faded quickly in the chilled air.

Jonah nodded. "Let's move."

They exited through the rear and circled back to the front. Wind howled between buildings. Reaper scanned from above, still on the fire escape. Nothing moved.

Then his voice came over comms.

"Six incoming. Fast. Down the street, to your left."

Jonah's eyes narrowed.

"Weapons hot. Hold the line. Get ready to engage."

CHAPTER 29

Wind thundered through broken windows and down empty streets, swirling litter in dusty eddies. Echo Black paused at the corner where Oak Avenue met East Seventh. Abandoned cars formed a crude blockade under flickering streetlamps. Beyond them, snow-dusted every rooftop, glinting in shifting shadows.

Jonah stared down the street. Across the barricade, six figures stepped into the lamplight. They stood nearly ten feet tall, gangly but muscular, hair tangled with a mix of earth and blood. Their broad foreheads and pronounced brow ridges gave them a Neanderthal appearance, primal and ancestral. Three formed a line up front, three behind, spacing perfect.

Ramirez crouched behind a hedge. His shotgun muzzle peered around the rim. Jenkins crouched near a short brick wall, shotgun at the ready. Havoc knelt behind a sedan, fingers tightening on his LAMG. Reaper watched from a second-floor fire escape off to their right, muzzle hugging cold steel railing.

Jonah raised a hand. "Six, all tall variety. Ramirez left. Jenkins right. Havoc, support from center. Reaper, overhead."

No one spoke. The beasts advanced in slow, deliberate steps. One gripped a twisted street sign like a spear. Each crunch of ice underfoot sounded exceptionally loud in the sudden stillness.

Jonah's finger brushed the trigger. "Now Reaper."

Reaper exhaled. His rifle barked. The first round punched through the leading creature's chin, shattering bone and sending dark rivulets down its neck. It staggered back, snarling, eyes wild.

Havoc opened up. The LAMG's thunder rattled windows.

Rounds tore into its chest, splintering ribs. The beast reeled, then fell, collapsing onto the frozen ground with a wet thud.

Jonah advanced into the gap. He zipped off two precise bursts into the second creature's temple. Its head snapped back, then rolled lifeless to the side.

Four remained.

The third beast lunged at Havoc's left flank, swinging the sign spear with brutal force. Metal screamed on impact as Havoc rolled clear. He dumped two rounds into its knee. Bone shattered. The creature twisted, dropping the spear with a clang that echoed down the block. Before it could rise, Jonah stepped forward and ended it with two shots to the skull.

Four down. Two still moving.

The fifth Sasquatch vaulted the barricade of cars. It landed inside Jonah's arc, swinging its monstrous arms. Jonah ducked and rolled left. The beast's hand skimmed his vest, crushing side pouches but missing ribs. Jenkins took a deep breath and fired. His round hit the creature's forearm, barely slowing it.

Ramirez pumped his shotgun. The bead sight locked on the beast's knee. One blast tore away muscle. The leg wobbled. Jonah regained stance and nailed a headshot. The Sasquatch did a pirouette before collapsing awkwardly to the ground.

Only one remained.

It roared in rage and picked up the stop-sign from the

frozen dirt. Frothing at the mouth, it raised the pole and charged Havoc. Havoc swung the LAMG but the ammo belt rattled empty. He ditched the weapon and drew his sidearm, a Glock ten-millimeter. Shots rang but the creature kept coming.

Jenkins saw it lining up the pole like a lance. He broke cover and sprinted at an angle, shouting to pull its focus. The beast turned, hurling the sign. Jenkins dove, but the red octagon edge sliced deep into his thigh. He screamed and toppled, instantly grabbing at his bloody leg.

Jonah sprinted. Ramirez followed. The Sasquatch tried to snatch Havoc but he rolled and emptied five rounds into its throat at point-blank range. It jerked, releasing a choking cough, then staggered toward Jonah.

Reaper's rifle cracked again. The bullet slammed into the base of its skull. The creature dropped, sliding on ice until it settled against a curb.

Silence swept the block, broken only by Jenkins' ragged breaths.

Jonah kneeled at Jenkins' side. The stop-sign pole had pierced high through muscle but missed the artery. Blood ran, yet the pulse was strong. Ramirez was already applying pressure. Jonah snapped a tourniquet above the wound, then tore open a packet of quick clot and packed it firmly into the gash.

Havoc slapped a fresh belt into his LAMG and secured the perimeter, scanning for secondary threats. Reaper climbed down the fire escape, landing in a crouch and walking over to Jonah.

Jenkins clenched teeth, sweat mixing with freezing air. "Not… my best night," he mumbled.

Jonah offered a tight smile. "You'll walk out. Might curse a few hundred times, but you'll walk."

CHAPTER 30

Snow blanketed the shattered skeleton of Duluth, softening its brutal ruin but hiding none of it. Buildings were smashed, their guts spilling into the streets.

Aluk stood in the middle of the street, shoulders hunched, his breath rising in slow plumes. His body was carved by the night's violence. Blood matted the hair on his forearms. Shards of glass jutted from his shoulder and cheek, catching the faint light. His face bore deep lacerations, one cutting across his brow where the empty socket wept with slow, dark fluid. Another cluster of embedded glass glinted beneath his jaw. He did not pull them free. He wore the wounds like war medals.

Behind him, Matto crouched and lowered his massive palm to the cold ground. His long fingers spread wide across the ice-dusted surface. He inhaled. In the same breath, he caught their scent, hairless ones. Close. Huddled. Maybe half a dozen. The tang of their fear cut through the cold.

Matto clicked low in his throat, a warning. He turned and chattered toward Aluk, brushing two fingers down his chest, then flicking them toward the west. They had done enough here. They should move on.

Aluk didn't answer with sound. His head tilted slightly, and an image burst between them, shared not through words but instinct. The memory of his father crushed beneath one of the hairless ones' metal beasts. The shriek of twisted limbs. The silence that followed.

Aluk's lips peeled back. He snarled.

Matto lowered his hand and stood still, the muscles in his legs taut. He let out a chattering exhale, but he knew there would be no stopping the leader now.

Aluk surged forward. He moved with purpose, his feet crunching through scattered debris and iced-over glass. He passed a toppled bus with blood smeared down its windows and ducked through a broken archway where the front door of the building had been torn off. He climbed with powerful, agile movements, using balconies like rocks. From the third level, he scanned the shadows below.

They were there. Huddled. Six of them. Various shapes

and sizes. They had crude weapons that would do them no good. Not against his kind. The hairless one's eyes were wide, faces streaked with blood and frozen tears. They didn't see him. But they could smell him.

Behind and below, Matto growled low, the sound rolling like thunder against the wind. He spread his fingers in a pushing gesture. Let them go. Move on. This was wasteful.

Aluk turned his head slowly and met Matto's eyes. He said nothing. Then he jumped.

The leader hit the ground like a landslide, sending snow and ice spinning into the air. The hairless ones barely had time to scream before he was among them. Matto closed his eyes.

The sounds that followed were sharp and brutal. Bone striking wall. Skin against tile. A scream cut short. The crashing of furniture flung into walls. A heavy body thrown through a window.

Matto stood in place, silent. His chest rose and fell with each breath, but he did not go near.

A moment later, Aluk stepped from the ruins. Hair slick with red, his shoulders heaving slightly. He dragged a hairless one behind him. Blood dripped from his forearm, steaming in the snow.

He looked at Matto. The message in his single eye was clear. Weakness had no place here. Mercy had been discarded long ago.

Matto said nothing. He turned and moved through the snow. Aluk followed, dragging the unconscious hairless one and soon led the way.

CHAPTER 31

The snow deepened as Aluk and Matto crossed into a narrower street flanked by ruined storefronts and cracked lampposts. Slumped cars lined the edges, half-buried, their windshields punched inward. The stench of blood lingered, but the trail here was colder.

Aluk dragged the limp body of the hairless one behind him, its limbs scraping frozen asphalt. As they slowed, he stopped and looked ahead. Then, with a sharp flick of his arm, he tossed the body aside. It landed with a dull thud against the base of a telephone pole, forgotten.

Matto's eyes tracked the motion, then shifted forward.

Ahead, four figures moved through the wreckage. Towering, broad-shouldered, coated in snow and blood, they were like Aluk and Matto, kin not of their clan but of their kind. One stepped forward, his hair streaked silver, body scarred from many winters. This one had been a leader once.

They stopped when they saw each other. No greeting came. Only breath misting in the cold.

The silver-haired one raised a flat hand. His fingers flicked outward, then downward. The signal was clear. Enough. It is done.

He took a step forward, his other hand clenching over his chest, then motioned toward the woods with a backward sweep. The others behind him mirrored the gesture. They were leaving. They had seen what Aluk's revenge had become.

Aluk didn't move. He stood tall, his chest rising, the glass in his skin catching what little light remained. The blood in his hair had dried. He looked like something risen from old myth, forged from frost and death.

Matto tensed. He stretched his shoulders. He grunted low in warning.

Aluk raised his hand, not to the others but toward Matto. In his mind, a vivid image burst like thunder. Hair scorched by fire. Food being taken out of their forest by hairless ones.

The message was rage.

The silver-haired one stepped closer, unfazed. He grunted and tapped his chest with three quick strikes. His hand swept across the broken city, then rose in a wide arc toward the sky. Too much. We dishonor what we are.

Behind him, one of the younger ones chuffed agreement, striking the ground with his palm. Another turned, already heading toward the edge of the forest.

Aluk's lips curled, teeth bared in a slow, menacing snarl.

Matto clicked sharply, swiping a claw through the air. Let it go.

But Aluk's reply came in motion.

He exploded forward.

The silver-haired Sasquatch barely shifted before Aluk slammed into him with the weight of a boulder. Their bodies collided, shaking snow from their wet hair. Aluk struck first, an elbow into the jaw, a swipe of his blood-caked forearm into the throat. The silver-haired one staggered but recovered, driving a massive knee into Aluk's ribs.

Matto backed away, heart hammering. The other two Sasquatch froze.

The fight turned brutal fast. They grappled, feet scraping

on icy ground, slamming each other into walls and frozen wreckage. Aluk ducked a swing and slammed the older one's head into the hood of a car. Metal groaned. He pulled back to strike again, but the silver-haired leader drove both fists into Aluk's sides and then raked his nails across Aluk's chest, reopening old wounds.

Aluk didn't retreat.

He threw himself forward, lifted the other off his feet, and slammed him onto the roof of a parked car. The metal caved. The impact sent a sharp crack through the air.

The silver-haired one rolled free, blood streaking his face. He clambered to his feet and charged, locking arms with Aluk once more. They twisted and slammed against each other, bodies clashing with the sound of meat on stone. Aluk bared his teeth and bit down, hard, into the other's shoulder. A deep, pulsing cry followed.

Matto turned his eyes away.

Another image rippled out from the silver-haired leader. His memories. Forest rituals. Young ones learning to climb. The warmth of safe darkness and clan unity.

The message was clear. We are not this.

Aluk's reply came as he spun the older one and drove him

hard into the frozen asphalt. He raised both fists and struck down. Once. Twice. A third time. The sounds were wet and final.

The leader stopped moving.

Aluk knelt there for a moment, hunched, breathing hard, hair tangled and slick with blood not his own. One of the other Sasquatch stepped forward, hands raised in trembling protest. Aluk rose and turned slowly. A deep growl rumbled from his chest, low and rattling.

They backed away.

No words. No grunts. Just the sound of their retreating steps in the snow.

Matto approached slowly, hands low, his body bowed in quiet deference. His eyes were not afraid but heavy. He gestured a slow arc across the ruined skyline, then crossed his arms over his chest. Vengeance no longer called. The path had changed.

Aluk turned his face skyward. Snow drifted onto the cuts that crisscrossed his flesh.

He looked back at Matto, eyes burning. A deep grunt rumbled from his chest, followed by sharp, chattering clicks. He slammed a fist against his chest, then thrust it toward the horizon.

"Come with me," his voice low and guttural, "or die like the rest."

CHAPTER 32

The basement was dim, lit only by a battery-powered lantern set on a table near the wall. The light threw long shadows across the concrete floor and the boxes stacked high against the window. Pete, the family's dog, lay near the kids, occasionally letting out a soft whine in his sleep.

No one had spoken for a while. Not since the last round of distant gunfire had faded out over an hour ago. The house above creaked now and then from the wind, but otherwise the world outside seemed to have gone still.

Zachariah sat on a blanket near the wall, elbows on his knees, gaze locked on the door at the top of the stairs. His face was tense.

Michael cleared his throat. "You guys don't sound like you're from around here."

Leon gave a small nod. "That's true. I'm from the Netherlands. And Wayne here is from the UK."

Wayne leaned back a little, his voice calm but worn. "Dragged him out here for the conference."

Leon chuckled. "I wanted to come too."

Wayne smirked. "Yeah, alright. I didn't have to drag him very hard."

Leon shrugged. "Truth be told, I've always been fascinated with cryptids. Just never thought I'd actually see a Sasquatch at a Sasquatch Conference."

Zachariah glanced over and gave a tired smile. "I don't think any of us did."

Then he looked toward the stairs again. "It's been quiet," he said. "Like, really quiet. I haven't heard anything in a long time."

The others looked up. Michael glanced toward the lantern, as if time might be hiding in its glow.

"I need to check on my mom," Zachariah said. "I've got to see if she's okay."

Leon sat up straighter. "Kid, I don't know if that's a good idea."

Zachariah shook his head. "I know it's not. But I can't just sit here. She's only a few streets away. I'll be quick."

Randy rubbed his forehead. "It's too dangerous."

"I'll be careful," Zachariah said. "I'm not dumb. I just… I gotta try."

He stood and turned to Michael. "Can I take the shotgun with me? I swear I'll bring it back if I make it."

Michael hesitated. He looked toward his kids, then towards the others. "I don't like the idea of you going at all," he said quietly. "But yeah. Take it."

Zachariah gave a small nod and headed to the stairs.

Randy stood as well. "Hell. I can't let the kid go alone."

Jenny sat up quickly. "Dad…"

"He's fifteen," Randy said. "I'd never forgive myself if something happened to him out there."

Jenny frowned. She looked at Zachariah, who was standing with his jaw set, hands gripping the shotgun tightly. Then she stood too. "Fine. We go with him. Make sure he's okay."

Randy had convinced Michael to loan him his prized

Mark XIX Desert Eagle .50. He turned to Michael. "We'll bring the guns back. Promise."

Michael nodded once. "Be smart. Don't try to be a hero."

Wayne and Leon stood just enough to see them off. "Good luck," Wayne said.

The three of them climbed the basement stairs, easing open the door to the hallway above.

It was quiet up there too. And cold.

Zachariah moved quickly to the front door and peaked out through its broken frame. They stepped outside, each of them watching the street.

The snow was deeper than before. Tire tracks and footprints were mostly gone now, covered over by the wind.

Zachariah led the way.

CHAPTER 33

The cold clung to everything as Zachariah, Randy and Jenny moved through backyards and side passages, each step muffled by snow-covered grass. Every fence creak and snapping twig jolted their nerves.

Zachariah gripped the shotgun tighter than he meant to. His gloves were damp from sweat. "She lives at the end of the cul-de-sac," he whispered. "Backs onto the woods. If she made it home from work, she's probably locked inside."

"Let's hope," Jenny said, her voice low and tight. She scanned every shadow. "I am going to need some serious therapy after this," she added.

Randy raised the Mark XIX Desert Eagle, sweeping his aim across the empty yards and parked cars. "Just stay low."

They slipped through a sagging fence, the crunch of their

boots the only sound. They hesitated before stepping out onto the Zachariah's street, a shadow rose from a clump of bushes in a nearby front yard.

A Sasquatch.

Zachariah froze. A cold chill gripped the base of his spine.

"Shit. Shit. What do we do?" Zachariah asked.

"Don't move. Just stay still," Randy said.

It loomed tall, at least eight feet. Its hair was soaked dark from the snow, hanging in thick strands, and its chest heaved as it locked eyes with them. Patches of its coat were crusted with blood, dried and fresh. It didn't charge. Instead, it growled low, the sound vibrating in their bones. The creature looked at their weapons, then back at them.

And stepped forward.

Its face twisted into something awful. A grin that wasn't a grin. Malicious. Predatory.

Zachariah stepped back, nearly tripping on a snow-covered rock. "It's gonna come at us," he whispered, trembling.

Jenny swallowed hard, trying to steady her hands. "Shoot if it does."

Before they could react, a sharp whistle cut through the stillness from the edge of the woods.

All four turned.

Another figure stepped out of the trees. Smaller. Maybe five feet tall. A juvenile Sasquatch, narrow and unsure. It whistled again, then grunted softly.

It walked with careful steps, shoulders slightly hunched, and a tremble in its limbs. Its hands twitched by its sides, and there was a flicker of fear in its wide, dark eyes.

The two began to communicate. Chatter, gestures, short grunts. The tall Sasquatch turned its head toward the small one, clearly irritated. It barked out something guttural. The small one flinched but didn't back down. It pointed toward Zachariah and the others, then flattened its palms and spread its arms wide.

Zachariah could feel his heart pounding in his ears. "It's trying to stop the big one," he whispered.

The larger Sasquatch snarled and squared its shoulders. It didn't back down.

Zachariah held his breath. Jenny shook uncontrollably.

Then the larger one roared and surged forward.

It snatched the juvenile by the neck and lifted it easily, holding it in the air. The smaller Sasquatch kicked and thrashed. The big one opened its mouth, lowering the young one toward its face.

A gunshot cracked through the cold.

The tall Sasquatch dropped. Legs went limp. The juvenile hit the ground and scrambled away on all fours.

Randy lowered the pistol slightly, exhaling.

The larger Sasquatch wasn't dead. It clawed at the ice-covered pavement, dragging its limp lower body behind. Its eyes flared with pain and rage. It snarled, blood bubbling at its lips.

Randy approached slowly. "Always wanted to fire one of these," he said, glancing at the gun. "Just never thought it'd be to shoot a Sasquatch."

The creature looked up at him, face contorted. Randy didn't hesitate. He aimed and pulled the trigger.

The bullet hit dead center.

Its head snapped backward, and the top half of its skull peeled open. Chunks of bone scattered across the snow, dark blood spraying in a wide arc. Its lower jaw hung crooked, split from the impact. One eye vanished completely in the mess. The body jerked once, then lay still.

"Hell of a recoil," Randy said as he rubbed his shoulder.

The juvenile Sasquatch had stopped a few feet away. It stared at Randy, breathing fast. Then it slowly raised its hands, palms flat and out.

Randy held the Desert Eagle ready but didn't move.

The juvenile backed up and headed back to the woods.

Zachariah's legs wobbled beneath him. "That was insane. I guess they aren't all monsters."

He looked down at the dead Sasquatch sprawled on the frozen ground. Blood pooled around its ruined skull, steaming faintly in the cold.

"They look ancient," he said quietly.

Jenny wiped at her face, trying to hide the shake in her hands. "Let's keep moving before something else shows up."

Randy looked down at the body, then up at the smaller one. "I agree."

The juvenile turned once at the edge of the woods. It held Randy's gaze for a long, unblinking second, then disappeared into the trees without a sound.

They didn't know his name.

But somewhere, long before this night, it had been given to him by his kind.

Brak.

CHAPTER 34

Their throats burned from the cold, every breath drawing air that felt like glass. Sweat from the earlier fight had dried into a clammy chill beneath their gear, leaving them raw and stiff as they walker deeper into the neighborhood.

Echo Black and the two officers moved in tight formation through a grid of snow-blanketed streets. Jonah led the way, rifle in hand, scanning every shadow twice. Jenkins limped along beside Ramirez, each step drawing a soft grunt. Reaper and Havoc followed behind, watching the flanks.

They were only three blocks from Ramirez's house.

He exhaled hard, voice quiet as he kept pace with the others. "My wife's probably got the kids huddled in the basement right now. No power. No way to reach anyone. I told her to keep the lights off and stay put, but that was hours ago."

They passed a burned-out SUV, its roof caved in and windows dusted with snow. A child's stuffed bear lay half-buried beside it, soaked and forgotten.

Jenkins grunted. "This place looked normal a day ago. Now it's like the whole city got swallowed."

Jonah raised a clenched fist and everyone froze. The silence deepened, broken only by boots creaking in packed snow and the distant snap of ice somewhere behind a fence. Something felt wrong. Stillness pushed in from every direction.

Jonah's eyes swept across the street. One yard over, a thick snowbank hugged the edge of the road. It looked like the others, dirty white and crusted with gravel.

"Everyone hold," Jonah said quietly.

Ramirez took a cautious step back. "What is it?"

Jonah didn't reply.

Then the snowbank exploded.

A massive form burst out in a spray of powder and debris. Gray-white hair and a roar that snapped the moment in two. The Sasquatch was already moving as it emerged, lunging forward with impossible speed and seizing Jenkins with one arm.

"Holy shit!" Ramirez shouted.

The creature turned and ran, dragging Jenkins like a doll. Jenkins kicked and struggled, cursing loud as the beast bounded toward the opposite curb.

Reaper reacted first.

He raised his rifle and fired once. The shot slammed into the Sasquatch high in the back, along the spine. It shrieked, a high, warbling sound that didn't belong in the human world, and its legs buckled mid-stride. Jenkins dropped from its grip and hit the ground hard, rolling before scooting backward out of reach.

The Sasquatch pitched forward into the curb. Its face hit with a heavy crunch, limbs flailing.

Havoc was already moving. He stepped in and fired a single round into the back of the creature's skull. The body shuddered and went still, blood pooling around the head.

Jenkins sat up, eyes wide, chest heaving. "That thing was about to drag me off and fucking eat me!"

Jonah reached for him. "You hurt?"

"No. Just freaked the fuck out." He stood slowly, limping a little more than before. "Didn't see a damn thing. Thought it was a snowdrift."

Ramirez helped him upright, glancing at the dead Sasquatch. "Neither did I. Blended in too well."

The creature's hair was almost the same color as the snowbank, white with streaks of ash and dirt. Against the curb and under shadow, it had been invisible. Only instinct had given Jonah pause.

"It waited," Havoc said. "That was a setup. Lucky it was us that came by and not civilians."

"Ain't that right?" Reaper added, checking his rifle. "Smart buggers."

Jonah didn't argue. He was already checking their surroundings. "Let's move."

They re-formed, rifles and shotguns up, and passed the body without another word. No one needed to speak. The lesson was already burned into their minds. In this new war, even the snow could hide an enemy.

They kept moving.

Three blocks to go.

CHAPTER 35

The house looked untouched. Snow-blanketed the porch in a smooth, shallow layer. Zachariah stepped off the sidewalk, shotgun gripped tight in both hands. His mom's car sat parked just off-center in the driveway, front bumper nearly brushing the steps. The angle said everything, it had been a rushed arrival.

Randy followed behind him, Desert Eagle in hand, scanning the quiet street. Jenny kept her distance near the gate, eyes darting across the neighboring yards.

Zachariah stepped onto the porch, breath clouding the air, and knelt to lift the doormat. The spare key was still there. Cold and a little dusty, but untouched. He unlocked the front door slowly and pushed it open with care.

The hallway inside was dim and still. Coats on the rack. Boots by the wall. Everything exactly as he remembered. But too quiet.

"Mom?" His voice echoed down the corridor. "It's me. It's Zachariah!"

No response.

Randy and Jenny stayed just behind him, stepping carefully through the doorway. "Living room first," Randy mumbled.

They swept the house room by room, finding nothing. Lights off. Kitchen empty. Back door locked. But something didn't feel right. Zachariah stopped outside the basement door. He leaned in and listened.

A sound. Soft. Scraping.

Then a low bark.

"Sigurd?" Zachariah called out. He turned the knob slowly. The door creaked open.

Randy raised his weapon and held position as Zachariah took the stairs down fast, two at a time.

A flashlight blinked on from the back corner of the basement. There she was. His mom, huddled under a heavy blanket, crouched between two familiar shapes. Sigurd and Freya barked once each before bounding toward him. Cyrus, their gray cat sat perched on a storage bin nearby, staring unbothered.

Zachariah dropped the shotgun and fell to his knees. His arms wrapped around both dogs, burying his face in Freya's fur. Sigurd licked at his cheek and whined loudly.

"Zachariah?" his mom said from behind them, her voice shaking. "Is it really you?"

Zachariah nodded and stepped forward. He stood and pulled her into a hug, wrapping both arms tight around her. "I'm here. I'm okay."

She pressed her face against his shoulder and let out a deep, broken breath. Her shoulders trembled as she held him. "I saw the videos online. Heard the reports. I left work and just drove. I didn't know what else to do. I came straight home and hoped you'd be here. I couldn't get through to anyone. My phone froze. The signal cut out."

Zachariah swallowed hard, eyes stinging as tears welled up. "I've been with some new friends I met at the conference," he said.

Randy and Jenny slipped into the basement quietly, eyes scanning the space before settling on Zachariah's mom. "Looks like you were smart about hiding," Jenny said gently.

"I didn't have much of a choice," she replied. "I heard the screams outside. The news said to stay low before it cut off. So I came down here with the dogs and cat. They didn't leave my side."

Freya nosed at her hand while Sigurd flopped against Zachariah's leg, tail thumping steadily.

"Thank you for helping my son. You are welcome to stay here until it is safe to leave," Zachariah's mother said quietly.

Randy nodded toward the small window. "Thanks. We'll stay here until we get the all-clear. Safer down than up." He gave Jenny a big hug, holding her close for a moment before letting go.

Zachariah leaned against the wall, both dogs beside him. His mother gripped his hand tightly, eyes still wet but steadier now.

Randy and Jenny settled on storage bins and folded blankets.

The air was tense but less frantic. Somewhere in the distance, they could hear faint sirens winding down.

CHAPTER 36

The group moved in tight formation, heads on a swivel. Their breath steamed in the frigid air, mixing with the faint scent of blood, metal and powder. Jonah led the way, eyes scanning each rooftop and alleyway. The silence wasn't peaceful. It sat heavy, unnatural.

Jenkins limped heavily, his face etched with exhaustion and pain. Ramirez flanked him, every few steps glancing over his shoulder. Reaper brought up the rear, his rifle angled toward the buildings. Havoc had the LAMG slung low, ready, his eyes sweeping back and forth. Every one of them knew what this kind of quiet meant.

They were only two blocks from Ramirez's home.

Cold settled deep in their joints, a creeping ache that made each step harder. Their throats were dry and raw, the sting of breathing in the freezing air after exertion.

The first rock came out of nowhere. It smashed against the curb just feet from Jonah, exploding in a shower of icy chips.

"Contact left!" Reaper shouted, swinging his weapon around.

More rocks followed, some the size of basketballs, crashing into nearby cars and walls with vicious force.

Havoc grunted as a rock slammed into his thigh. He stumbled, pain shooting up his leg, but he stayed upright, raising his LAMG and returning fire toward the shadows. Muzzle flashes lit the block in bursts as the team and officers spread out, scanning the rooftops and shadows.

Ramirez and Jenkins moved to cover, weapons up. "They're all around us!" Ramirez yelled.

Jonah moved forward through the hail of rocks and bullets. Then he saw three Sasquatch emerging from behind a bus, ducking and weaving with surprising speed. They threw with violent intent, snarling as more rocks soared.

Reaper dropped the first one with a clean shot to the throat. It crumpled mid-lunge. Havoc pivoted and gunned down the second as it tried to flank them near a rusted-out pickup.

A sudden whack cracked against the ground just ahead of them. A basketball-sized chunk of concrete shattered, spraying chips. Another rock crashed into the side of a parked sedan, caving the door in with a metal crunch. Havoc stumbled back, a third rock striking his upper thigh with enough force to drop him to one knee.

"Contact!" Reaper shouted, pivoting toward the source.

The street erupted into chaos. From the snowbanks and ruined storefronts, figures rose, gray and white, massive, blending into the ice and snow like phantoms. Five in total, each one over ten feet tall, hunched and snarling. Their eyes burned amber in the dim light. The ambush was well-coordinated, and they'd waited for the exact moment when tension started to ebb.

Havoc rose back up, his face twisted in pain but still in the fight. He leveled the LAMG and sprayed a controlled burst at the nearest beast. Rounds tore into its chest, flinging chunks of hide and muscle. The Sasquatch collapsed with a gurgled shriek.

Reaper fired next, a clean triple-tap into the head of another creature sprinting toward them from behind a pile of crates. It dropped mid-lunge, crashing through a chain-link fence with a rattling thud.

Jonah dropped to one knee and fired into the shoulder of a third. The beast roared and veered left, running straight into Ramirez, who blasted a shell from his shotgun point-blank into its gut. The creature folded, spewing dark blood across the pavement.

Another Sasquatch tried to leap down from a rooftop. Jenkins caught it mid-air with a slug to the chest. The creature landed badly, flailed, then was finished off by Reaper's follow-up shot to the skull.

Four down.

The final one tried to flee, howling as it turned and darted down an alley. Jonah raised his rifle and fired a single round. It punched through the back of the creature's neck and sent it tumbling forward into the slush.

The street went quiet for just a beat.

Then Aluk stepped from behind a wrecked car.

Jonah stared up, heartbeat quickening. One good eye glared back at him, burning amber in the dark. Glass cuts marked the Sasquatch's bare chest and shoulders, wounds still fresh. The scars gleamed in the moonlight like jagged frost. The hair across his shoulders was patchy, scorched and thinned from fire.

It took Jonah only a second to place him.

This was the one from Devil's Track Lake. The lead Sasquatch. The one who had stared him down through smoke and pine trees. The one who had lived.

Aluk straightened, rising to his full height in the middle of the road. Snow clung to his back and shoulders. He was breathing hard, nostrils flaring as he stared directly at Jonah. He sniffed the air, then bared his teeth. He recognized the scent.

Jonah started to raise his rifle.

Aluk's arm moved in a blur. A rock spun through the air with unnatural speed. It struck Jonah's rifle squarely, knocking it from his hands and sending it clattering to the icy ground.

Jonah cursed and dove behind a car as Aluk charged, boots slapping on the ice as he ran.

"Shit!" he mumbled, spinning to run.

Aluk bellowed, thundering after him.

Jonah vaulted a mangled delivery truck, cut through a narrow alley, and slid over a hood crusted in ice. He could feel Aluk closing behind him, hear the labored breath, the heavy steps.

"Going for the station up ahead," he rasped into his mic, breath ragged. "Havoc, light it up when he's inside."

A low snarl echoed behind him. Not rage. Not pain. Something worse.

Enjoyment.

Aluk was toying with him.

Jonah bolted across the street toward the old gas station. Its roof sagged, the front wall half collapsed, a Sasquatch already lying dead on the cold ground. He slipped through the doorway and into the gloom, boots crunching glass and debris.

Behind him, Aluk roared and barreled inside.

From outside, Havoc was already aiming.

"Two going in!" he shouted into his mic.

"Confirmed," Reaper replied. "Clear to fire."

Two grenades launched with thudding coughs.

The launcher's thump was deafening. A second one followed.

The gas station erupted in a wall of fire and glass.

Jonah burst through the back as the blast lifted him off his feet. Heat surged behind him, followed by a concussive wave that flattened everything in a ten-yard radius.

Inside, Aluk was hurled backward like a ragdoll caught in a tornado. His body flew through the flames and wreckage, arms flailing, one last roar ripping from his throat. He struck a jagged steel rod jutting from the collapsed awning frame, the force driving it through his back and out his chest. His momentum carried him down the shaft until his massive frame hung limp, impaled, smoke rising from scorched hair and blackened skin.

The ground vibrated long after the shockwave faded.

Smoke curled around the twisted ruin.

Jonah rose slowly from behind the dumpster, heart pounding, skin stung from flying grit and heat. The gas station was now a crater of flame and rubble. The metal sign had warped, the walls were gone, and debris continued to fall like ash.

Jonah limped forward, trying to control his breathing. He stared at the motionless body.

Reaper and Havoc joined him a moment later.

"You good?" Reaper asked.

Jonah didn't answer right away. He stared at the ruin, watching the flames dance through what was left of Aluk's hair.

"Yeah," he said at last. "He's cooked."

They stood in silence as the fire crackled and wind swept ash across the street.

"Let's get the hell out of here," Jonah said.

Havoc sniffed and wrinkled his nose. "Yeah, it smells like Sasquatch BBQ."

The street around them fell quiet. Just the crackle of fire and the distant groan of a collapsing beam. The war had left its mark, and the leader of the uprising was dead.

Across the street, high on a snow-covered hill overlooking the smoldering wreckage, another figure stood motionless. Broad, with long arms and thick gray-brown hair, it watched the men in silence.

He had seen Aluk die. He had watched the flames take him, seen the twisted body impaled and broken. And he was glad. There had been too much blood, too much pride in the killing. Aluk had led them to ruin.

Slowly, he turned and disappeared into the trees.

Matto was gone before any of them ever saw him.

CHAPTER 37

Ramirez didn't wait. As soon as the street opened up ahead, he broke into a run, boots slipping slightly on ice as he turned onto a quiet block lined with dark houses and snow-covered yards. His breaths came in short bursts, each one fogging in the frigid air. Sweat clung to the back of his neck beneath his collar.

The night of terror, gunfire, and blood had worn him raw, and now his only thought was of the people inside the modest two-story brick house halfway down the block.

"Hold up," Reaper called, catching up. "I'm going in with you. Just in case."

Ramirez didn't argue. He nodded once and kept moving. Lights were off in the house. The front door was closed, undisturbed. He reached the porch, heart pounding harder now than it had during the firefight. Reaper stepped in beside him, rifle angled low.

Ramirez used a spared key to unlock the door.

He pushed it open, stepping into the quiet gloom of the hallway. "Maria?" he called. "It's me."

No response.

Reaper checked the living room while Ramirez moved deeper inside, sweeping the hallway with his sidearm. A noise came from upstairs, small, quick footsteps. Then a familiar voice.

"Dad?"

Ramirez exhaled, knees almost giving. "Emily. Where's your mom?"

"Upstairs with Mateo. We've been hiding."

Reaper stayed near the stairs while Ramirez bounded up, taking them two at a time. A second later, his shout echoed down. "They're okay. All of them."

Reaper allowed himself a smile and lowered his weapon.

Out on the street, Jonah dug his phone out of his pocket, raising it as it vibrated. "Briggs, this is Command."

He stepped away from the sidewalk, eyes still sweeping

the nearby roofs and alleys. "Go for Briggs."

"You're clear to stand down. Ninety-five percent of Duluth is secure. We've got drones in the air scanning for stragglers. Good work."

Jonah let out a breath he hadn't realized he was holding. "Appreciate the update."

"A vehicle is enroute to your location for exfil. Should reach you in ten."

"Copy that," Jonah replied. "Echo Black will be ready."

He lowered his phone and looked back at the house where Ramirez's silhouette now stood in the window, a small child clinging to him.

The wind tugged at his jacket. Snow continued to fall in a quiet hush, but the violence of the night no longer echoed through the streets. The silence was different now, no longer ominous. Just tired.

Havoc approached from down the block, dragging his LAMG with him.

"They okay?" he asked, voice rough with fatigue.

"They're safe," Jonah said.

"Good." Havoc dropped the weapon onto the hood of a car and leaned against it. "We need food, sleep and to get our asses to Texas."

Jonah nodded, eyes still fixed on the house. "Agreed."

Havoc shifted, cracking his neck. "What do you think they're gonna do with all the bodies?"

Jonah didn't answer right away. His gaze drifted toward the tree line.

"They'll be gone before the sun is fully up," he said. "What they do with them after that is anyone's guess."

Reaper stepped out of the house and joined them, his rifle resting against his shoulder.

"They've already got enough of them to study," he said. "They'll just burn them, no doubt."

No one argued. The snow kept falling.

CHAPTER 38

The sirens came first, distant at first, then closer. A pair of them, rising and falling through the cold air like a promise. Michael's hand tightened around the rifle he had carried for hours. His shoulders ached from holding it ready for too long, sweat cold against his back despite the chill.

Leon and Wayne sat on boxes near the back wall, quiet and still. Wayne's hands rested on his knees, his eyes trained on the ceiling above. Leon leaned forward slightly, head down, elbows on his thighs. They both had blankets draped over their shoulders.

Michael stood from where he had been keeping watch near the basement door. He turned and checked on his kids, who were curled up together in a makeshift bed of blankets and coats. Pete the dog lay asleep beside them, his chest rising and falling in steady rhythm. Their faces were peaceful, mouths parted in sleep. Somehow, they had fallen asleep a while ago.

He let out a slow breath, then turned to Leon and Wayne. "I'll go check."

Wayne rose slowly. "I'll come with you."

Leon gave a nod and stood as well. "We should all go."

They moved up together, the stairs groaning under their weight. Michael led, rifle cradled close to his chest. At the top, he pushed aside the damaged front door. Hinges groaned faintly.

Two police cruisers sat partway down the block, lights pulsing over the frost-covered street. One officer stood in the open, talking into a radio, while the other leaned against the hood, scanning both sidewalks, rifle raised. A few neighbors stepped out from their homes, quiet and tentative, some with bats or guns clutched in tight grips.

Leon stepped beside Michael. "It must be over," he said, voice low.

Wayne let out a long breath. "Thank God."

Michael said nothing, eyes never leaving the cruisers. The rifle stayed in his hands, though the barrel lowered a little.

Leon turned to him, his expression raw. "Thank you for letting us stay. I don't know what would've happened if you had said no."

Wayne gave a single nod. "Seriously. You didn't have to take us in, but you did. I just hope Zachariah, Jenny and Randy made it ok."

Michael gave a nod. "Me too."

Leon looked around at the neighbors stepping out into the open, faces uncertain in the flashing red and blue. "What a hell of a crazy welcome to the USA."

Wayne nodded. "Yeah, I don't think we need to go to Bluff Creek anymore. Pretty sure we've seen enough of them up close and way too damn personal."

Leon glanced at him and chuckled. "Yeah, straight home to a bottle of whiskey and a padded room."

They stood quietly together as the cold wind moved down the street, stirring loose leaves and snow. The only sounds now were the hum of engines and the distant creak of a shattered world beginning to settle.

CHAPTER 39

Michael didn't hear the car pull up. He was too focused on the mess. The cold inside the house bit through his flannel shirt, a deep chill that crept into his bones. The broken sliding door at the back of the house had turned his living space into a walk-in freezer. He'd taped thick blankets across the opening to block the worst of it, but the wind still pushed through the gaps. He'd need to get wood later, something solid to seal it off.

The Sasquatch lay sprawled across both the kitchen and the living room. One massive arm stretched over the broken tiles, the other into the carpet. Blood had soaked into both surfaces, dark and sticky. The thing's jaw was shattered, and its eyes had rolled back into its skull. Hair was matted and filthy, the smell hanging heavy in the air.

Michael swept the last of the glass into a dustpan,

breathing through his mouth to avoid the worst of the stench.

The front door creaked open behind him. He turned just as Eric stepped into the house.

"Jesus," Eric said, wide-eyed. "Your alive!"

Michael nodded and leaned the broom against the counter. "Yeah brother. Kids are asleep upstairs. Pete's with them."

Eric rubbed his hands together and looked around. "You got a freezer open in here?"

"Back door's gone. Blankets are just a temporary fix."

Eric's eyes fell on the body sprawled across the two rooms. He stepped closer, taking in the massive legs, the thick torso and the battered head.

"Holy hell. You actually killed one." he said.

"Came through the back glass doors last night. Took a few rounds to drop it."

Eric let out a long breath and stared at it. "Damn thing's enormous."

"You're telling me."

Eric crouched to get a better look, then stood again quickly. "It smells like a bear crawled through a septic tank and died."

Michael smirked. "You're not wrong."

Eric circled the creature once, hands on hips. "What are we even doing here, Mike? I mean seriously. You got a damn Bigfoot in your kitchen."

"I'm not calling anyone. You know how this'll go," Michael said.

He walked over and looked down at the body, his voice low. "You can bet they are already pretending this didn't happen. You think the government's going to own up to this? Admit a species like this exists? Not a chance."

Eric narrowed his eyes. "You're saying we're keeping this?"

"I'm saying we move it to the garage and preserve it. Long enough to find someone who won't lie through their teeth about it."

Eric looked from the body to his brother, then back again. "That thing has to weigh seven hundred pounds, easy."

"I'd say closer to eight," Michael replied.

Eric gave a slow nod. "Alright. So we're just two guys moving a dead cryptid. You got a forklift hiding out there?"

"I've got something better. The cherry picker."

Eric blinked. "The engine hoist? You're kidding."

Michael opened the door to the garage. "It worked on that engine block."

"Yeah and nearly dropped it on your foot."

"I reinforced it."

Eric sighed. "Let's say we get it up. Where are we putting it?"

"The workbench will hold."

"I dunno. That bench is sturdy, but this isn't a carburettor. It's a fucking monster with thighs the size of tree trunks."

Michael grabbed the hoist from the corner and wheeled it over. "You want to help or keep cracking jokes?"

Eric grinned. "Both, ideally."

He paused, then added, "You know I use humor when I'm nervous. I've been worried all night about you and the kids."

Michael glanced at him, a tired smile tugging at the corner of his mouth, then reached out and gave his shoulder a firm pat.

Getting to work, they looped chains around the creature, careful not to get too close to its grisly head.

"I swear if this thing twitches, I'm out that door," Eric said.

"It's not twitching. It's dead."

"Right. Just checking. Because if it even breathes weird, I'm putting a hole in the roof getting out of here."

They strained, cursed, and grunted their way through lifting it. The cherry picker groaned, but it held. The creature swayed under the hoist like some horrific carnival prize.

Eric steadied the leg as they rolled it into the garage. "We really doing this?"

Michael nodded. "We are."

They settled the body onto the workbench, packed ice around the chest and skull, and stepped back.

Eric shook out his arms. "You know we're both crazy, right?"

Michael looked at the lifeless creature. "Maybe. But now we've got proof."

Eric nodded slowly. "I've seen some crap in my day. But this? This takes the cake."

The garage was silent for a few seconds. Then Michael spoke.

"Thanks for showing up."

Eric shrugged. "Yeah, well. I figured if anyone was gonna survive a monster attack, it'd be you. With a gun and a plan."

Michael laughed once, tired and short. "Not much of a plan."

"Better than most people had."

Outside, the sun had risen just past the trees, lighting the ice on the garage windows. The crows had quieted. No more sirens. Just cold air and the sound of two brothers catching their breath beside the body of a legend.

EPILOGUE

James Jackson eased back into the wicker chair on his rear porch, dawn tinting a low ceiling of cloud the color of iron. Fine flakes drifted sideways across the field, settling on the sleeve of his jacket and on the walnut stock of the shotgun resting against the rail. The fresh cigar in his fingers glowed with each pull, its sweet smoke climbing into air that smelled of pine, gunpowder, and scorched hair.

A small battery-powered radio crackled to life on the table beside him.

"Residents in eastern Duluth can breathe a little easier," the announcer said, voice composed and bright. "National Guard units are on scene. No new sightings in the past hour, but authorities urge vigilance. Keep phone lines clear for emergencies."

She spoke of nine-one-one operators overwhelmed

before the system collapsed, of repair crews now patching the grid street by street. Not once did she say Bigfoot or Sasquatch. They were only wild creatures in her careful script, as if she had been told not to mention those words.

James exhaled a ribbon of blue-gray smoke and let his gaze travel over the winter grass. Two blackened shapes lay at least two hundred fifty yards beyond the porch, half embedded in a crust of new snow. Claymore mines had done their work, peeling hide and muscle to charcoal. The wind shifted, carrying a rancid mix of burned meat and singed hair back toward the house. Even at that distance he could taste it on the air.

The announcer repeated evacuation numbers and emergency contacts, then cut to a recorded briefing from a state wildlife officer. James let the words wash over him while the memory returned. He could still picture the creature's hand reaching in through his bedroom window, long, dark fingers curling past the frame, nails as thick as shed antlers.

He raised the cigar and tasted the leaf again. Snow whispered against the porch roof. He considered clearing the remains before snow buried them, then dismissed the idea. Better to leave the warning visible. Any other giants that strayed from the timber would see the black smears against the pale field and think twice.

Across the yard a crow fluttered down, eyed the carnage, and hopped away in jerky fits of caution. James ground ash into the tray and listened as the broadcast shifted to soft instrumental music, violin and piano bleeding through faint static. He turned the volume low. The melody sounded oddly fragile against the hush of falling snow.

He stood, joints stiff, and slung the shotgun over one shoulder. Another draw on the cigar warmed his lungs. The music continued behind him, thin notes searching for something untouched. Out in the drifting white the ruined bodies lay silent proof of what had happened here, and of what could happen again.

James watched the field until his breath turned the air to fog. Then he spoke to no one at all, voice clear and low.

"They say to leave a breathing tongue to shout the fear. I spared no one, yet Duluth has heard it loud and clear."

ABOUT THE AUTHOR

 Luka T. Jacobs, an author from the picturesque Illawarra region south of Sydney, Australia, is passionate about cryptids like Sasquatch and Dogman. She lives there with her partner and their dog, Finnigan.

Luka's love for animals and adventure fuels her storytelling. With a background in Graphic Design and Art, she adds a unique visual flair to her work. An avid traveler and explorer, she draws inspiration from the wild, eager to share her imaginative worlds with readers.

Luka T. Jacobs

STAY CONNECTED AND JOIN THE CONVERSATION!

FB: https://www.facebook.com/lukatjacobs
A: https://amazon.com/author/lukatjacobs
W: http://www.LukaTJacobs.com

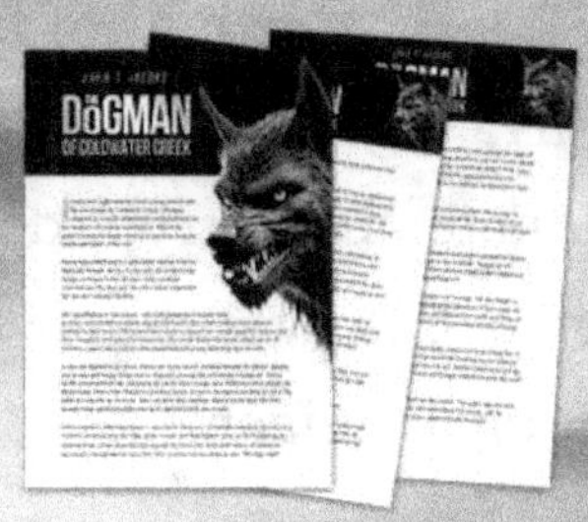

JOIN CRYPTID HORROR CENTRAL

Join my email list and get first access to new releases and download my **FREE** short story *"The Dogman of Coldwater Creek"*.

WWW.LUKATJACOBS.COM

Dear Reader,

Thank you for choosing my book amidst a sea of choices,
it truly means the world to me.

If you enjoyed the story, I'd love it if you shared
your experience with others and left a review.
As an independent author, your voice helps bring
these tales to life for more readers, and every
recommendation makes a tremendous impact.

Thank you again for joining me on this journey.
I'm so grateful to have you as a reader!

SNEAK PEEK: CLASH OF THE CRYPTIDS PART 1

Barbara rinsed the last of the dinner dishes and set the damp towel over the oven handle. The clock on the microwave blinked 9:47. Joel had already gone to bed an hour ago, like clockwork, same as every night. He never said much after dinner. Just shuffled off with his bad knees and mumbled something about the early weather report.

She didn't mind. Joel wasn't the talkative type, and after twenty-eight years in the same modest home just outside of town, they'd found a rhythm that worked. He'd turn in early. She'd tidy up, double-check the doors, and finish the day with her quiet ritual, a smoke, and a single shot of whiskey out on the screened porch. Just one. It helped her sleep.

The back porch wrapped around the side of the house, screened in with old mesh and aluminium trim they'd replaced twice in the last decade. The boards creaked a little when she stepped out, but it was a familiar sound. A part of the house she trusted.

Barbara settled onto the old wicker sofa with its faded cushions and lit her cigarette. The glow of the cherry was soft in the dark. She sipped her whiskey, smooth and biting. Around her, the trees whispered in the distance. The land sloped down beyond their yard into a thin stretch of woods. Past that, fields and silence. The stars shimmered above the black outline of the ridge, and the porch light cast a dull yellow cone across the steps.

She breathed in the cool air. The house felt so much bigger now that the kids had all moved out, married, scattered. There were toys in other living rooms now. Pictures on other refrigerators. That was okay. Barbara had made her peace with it.

Tonight was colder than it had been all week. She pulled her cardigan tighter and listened to the chirping of night frogs, the dry clicking of crickets. A barred owl hooted once from deeper in the trees, long and low.

And then, all at once, everything stopped.

The silence didn't come gradually. It was as if the volume had been cut. One second, the night was alive. The next, it was hollow.

Barbara held her cigarette mid-air. She frowned and turned her head slowly, listening. Nothing. No rustling. No insects. Even the trees had gone still.

She looked out across the yard. Her eyes took a second to adjust. At first, she thought maybe it was a passing cloud overhead, but the stars were still there, clear and cold. The stillness wasn't above. It was all around.

She exhaled deeply, heart thumping in a way she hadn't felt in years. Unease settled in her chest like an extra weight.

Probably a fox. Or a coyote somewhere near. That would shut the others up.

Still, she couldn't shake the feeling of dread. Her cigarette burned low. She took another sip of whiskey, forcing her shoulders to relax. "Don't be ridiculous," she mumbled, and brought the cigarette back to her lips.

A pair of reddish-amber lights hovered at the edge of the trees, about sixty yards away. Low to the ground. She squinted, leaning forward a little.

Deer, maybe. But no, deer had eyes on the sides of their heads, and these were forward-facing. Flat. Focused. Like something watching. And there was no reflection from her porch light. They seemed to glow on their own.

She narrowed her eyes. The lights didn't move. Just hung there, motionless, about a foot off the ground.

They blinked.

Barbara froze. Her hand trembled slightly, whiskey sloshing in the glass. The cigarette burned down to her fingers before she noticed and cursed softly, stubbing it out in the old ashtray beside her. When she looked back up, her breath caught.

Three more pairs of eyes had appeared, flickering into existence two at a time, each as still and unnatural as the first.

She gripped the edge of the cushion, mouth dry. "Joel," she whispered, though she didn't move. Her legs felt rooted, but her instincts screamed to get inside.

The first set of eyes began to rise.

Not forward. Not closer. Up.

As they climbed, the air filled with a sickening crunch, wet and heavy, like bones being snapped into place. A sharp jolt of nausea shot through her chest.

She gasped and stumbled up from the sofa, one hand gripping the door frame. She yanked the door open with too much force. The mesh slapped as she rushed inside.

She slammed it shut, breathing hard.

Just before she turned to go, she looked once more through the screen.

The yard was empty.

No eyes.

No movement.

Just blackness.

She didn't realize she was crying until she reached the bedroom and stood in the doorway. Joel snored softly on his side of the bed, unaware. She wiped her face, heart pounding.

Maybe she had imagined it. Maybe the shadows had played tricks on her. Whiskey and nerves. She hadn't eaten much at dinner. That could do it.

But no matter how she spun it in her head, nothing added up.

She slid into bed beside Joel, staring at the ceiling for a long time before sleep finally came in shallow, twitchy waves.

It wouldn't last.

****

Something woke her.

Not a sound at first, but the absence of it. That same unnatural stillness seemed to stretch and settle over the house like a shroud. Barbara opened her eyes and stared at the ceiling, unsure of how long she'd been asleep. The room felt colder than it should have been.

She turned her head toward the window. The curtains hung still. But something shifted outside, a shadow, brief and low, slipping past the frame.

She sat up, frowning. Joel breathed deeply beside her, one arm sprawled across the blanket, undisturbed.

There. A sound this time. Light. Unmistakenly intentional.

Tap. Tap.

Barbara held her breath.

It came again.

Not at the bedroom window, but from somewhere else in the house. Farther off. She slipped out of bed and crept toward the hallway, easing the door open just wide enough to slip through. The boards under her feet were cool and slightly warped with age, but she knew how to walk them quietly.

Another sound. This time at the front of the house.

Scratch. Tap. A pause. Then two more taps. Not like fingers. Not like claws either. Something in between. The pattern suggested curiosity, but not quite.

She stepped into the living room. The porch outside was dark. No streetlamp reached them this far out, and the porch light had burned out sometime last week. She had forgotten to replace it. Shadows bent oddly along the far wall, the little light that remained in the room catching on furniture and picture frames. The curtains in the kitchen hung undisturbed.

She reached for the light switch but stopped. Her instincts told her no.

Outside, near the porch, came a long exhale. Wet, low, almost thoughtful.

Barbara's stomach tightened.

She moved back into the hallway and turned toward the kitchen. The back of the house was darker. The only glow was from the microwave clock. She stared at the numbers and couldn't read them, her eyes refusing to adjust.

Something passed in front of the kitchen window.

A shape. Brief. Tall. It wasn't just moving by. It was looking in.

Barbara ducked behind the corner and pressed a hand to her chest. Her pulse thudded against her ribs. She felt foolish hiding in her own home but knew, deep down, that whatever was out there wasn't passing through. It was waiting for something.

A heavy thud hit the back porch.

She jumped. The screen door creaked softly, the sound of weight pressing against it. Not opening. Testing.

Another set of footsteps, slower. Moving across gravel.

Then silence again.

Barbara backed into the dining room, not wanting to wake Joel unless she had to. Maybe it was kids. Maybe someone was screwing around. But even as the thought came, she dismissed it. This wasn't the sound of kids on a dare. This was colder. It felt… sinister.

A single knock echoed from the front door.

She stared at it. The knock was soft. Rhythmic.

Knock. Knock.

Like it understood what the door was for.

Her mouth went dry. She moved toward it slowly, keeping out of view of the side window. She reached the peephole and almost didn't look through, afraid of what she might see.

She forced herself to.

Nothing.

She waited, holding her breath.

Then movement at the far edge of the yard. Not directly at the door. Something walked along the side of the house, low and slow.

She stepped back from the peephole and turned toward the hallway. She didn't make it two steps before something slammed against the side wall, hard enough to rattle a picture frame.

She bit down a scream and dropped to a crouch, heart hammering.

Something hit the screen door next. Not a full impact, but the sound of something dragging across it. A hand or claws or something worse.

Joel stirred.

Barbara crawled down the hall and slipped back into the bedroom. Joel sat halfway up, squinting.

"What are you doing?" he whispered.

"Something's outside," she whispered back. "More than one."

He rubbed his face. "What do you mean, something?"

"I saw eyes earlier. Now they're testing the house."

He blinked, clearly trying to shake off sleep. "Get the shotgun."

She was already moving.

From the hall, a low scrape echoed again, like nails along plaster.

Joel mumbled something under his breath and moved to the window, peeking through a slit in the curtain.

Barbara returned with the shotgun and handed it off.

"Should I call the sheriff?" she asked.

Joel shook his head. "No. I can handle it. We've got this and shells in the drawer. Anything out there would be stupid to try and come inside."

The porch outside was still dark.

They waited.

Barbara gripped Joel's arm.

Across the house, something hit the screen porch again.

Then silence.

Then running.

Four sets of footsteps, bare, powerful, fast, circled the house in unison. Gravel kicked up. Boards creaked near the porch. Something knocked over the trash bins. Then another figure rushed past the side window, too fast to see clearly.

Barbara flinched and grabbed Joel's sleeve.

"What do they want?" she whispered.

Joel didn't answer.

He stepped forward, opened the back door, and fired the shotgun straight through the screen. The blast shattered the quiet.

For a second, there was nothing.

Then a howl.

Not a dog. Not anything she had ever heard. It carried a sound inside it like broken glass and rage. One of them was hurt.

Joel stared toward the porch. "Is that a wolf?"

Barbara shook her head slowly, voice low. "If it's wolves, then they've learned to walk on two freakin legs."

The others responded with a deep, guttural rumble that passed through the wood floor like thunder.

Joel reloaded. "Go get the rifle. Load it and stay alert."

Barbara moved toward the hallway where she could see both ends of the house.

Something skittered onto the roof.

She looked up, staring at the ceiling as faint vibrations moved through the rafters. Whatever it was walked slowly, not trying to hide anymore. It moved like it had no fear of what might wait below.

Joel raised the shotgun again.

"Don't," Barbara said. "Not unless it comes through."

Outside, the gravel shifted again.

This time, they heard a dragging sound. Like something pulling its own leg. The one Joel hit.

Barbara turned back toward the living room window, where the glass had started to fog at the edges.

She walked closer.

There were handprints on the glass.

Two of them.

Impossibly large. Smudged at the fingertips. Long streaks where claws had scraped across the surface.

****

The house had gone still again, but it wasn't peaceful. Every wall, every floorboard seemed to listen.

Joel stood at the window with the shotgun tucked tight against his shoulder. Barbara moved through the kitchen, her hands steady despite the tremble she could feel under her skin. She found the rifle in the hall closet, where it had gathered dust behind a stack of boots and an old tackle box. She loaded it quickly, relying on memory. She paused once to listen.

The dragging sound had stopped.

When she stepped back into the living room, Joel acknowledged her but didn't speak. His jaw was set, eyes fixed on the fogged glass. The handprints were still there, just beginning to fade. She didn't need to be told they were watching.

Another knock. This time from the side door near the laundry room.

Three knocks.

Barbara raised the rifle. Her mouth was dry, and her tongue felt too thick. Joel motioned her to the hallway while he took a step toward the door.

The knock came again. But this time, it wasn't wood.

It was screen. Thin and metallic, the high-pitched rattle of claws tracing the mesh in a slow circle. The door handle twitched. Not hard. A test.

Barbara felt something shift behind her. She turned toward the back porch.

A faint scrape. Something brushing against wood and torn metal.

Her breath hitched.

Joel turned too, eyes narrowing.

The screen door was still hanging off its frame, warped and half-shattered from the shotgun blast. It swayed slightly now, nudged by something outside.

Barbara raised her rifle and stepped quietly toward the kitchen. The dark beyond the window was impenetrable. The only thing she could see was her own reflection.

The solid wooden back door held firm and steady.

Joel stepped beside her, shotgun already aimed.

They could hear movement just beyond it. Not footsteps exactly. Weight shifting. Something dragging across the boards of the porch.

Then a breath.

Right on the other side. Wet. Slow. A sound like an animal savoring a scent.

Barbara watched the doorknob and froze when it twitched. Just a little. Just enough.

Joel gripped the shotgun tighter but didn't fire.

"If it comes through, then shoot," he said quietly. "Not

before."

Barbara nodded.

They waited.

From the far side of the house came the sound of claws scraping down the siding. Another moved fast, skimming past the living room windows and toward the front door.Joel backed away from the kitchen. "They're feeling us out."

Barbara moved to the front. Her hand trembled now, but the rifle stayed level. She stopped near the entryway, where the dark pressed against the glass like smoke.

A shape paused just beyond the edge of the porch. Tall. Too tall. Its outline shifted, and she thought she saw a head tilt.

It stepped forward into view.

Her first instinct was to shoot, but Joel's words held her. The creature didn't charge. It didn't retreat. It stood just outside the line of shadow, eyes glowing faintly from beneath a sloping brow. Its arms hung low, and its chest moved with a slow, steady rhythm. It blinked once, then moved its head in a slow arc, as if scanning the house.

Joel appeared beside her and raised the shotgun again.

"Wait," Barbara whispered.

The creature stepped backward, melting into the dark.

For a moment, they heard nothing but their own breath.

Then a sharp cry broke the silence. Not a howl this time. A yelp, shrill and sudden.

And just like that, they were gone.

No footsteps. No rustling. Nothing.

Barbara stood frozen, watching the windows. The fog on the glass cleared slowly, leaving only moisture and streaks behind.

Joel lowered the shotgun. "I think they got what they came for."

She took a deep breath she had been holding since it all began. "I hope so." Barbara replied. "I don't think I could take much more of this."

They checked the doors, reinforced the latches, pushed a chair under the front doorknob and stacked firewood behind the back one. Neither of them spoke.

An hour passed.

Then another.

They sat on the couch, side by side, weapons across their laps. The silence in the house felt thick, every creak, and shift of the wood carrying more weight than it should have.

Outside, the sounds of night returned one at a time.

Crickets first. Then the low hoot of an owl. Then a breeze moved through the trees, and it sounded like it always had.

But they didn't move.

They sat and listened, eyes fixed on the dark windows, too terrified to believe it was over. Too afraid to trust that whatever had come to their home had truly gone.

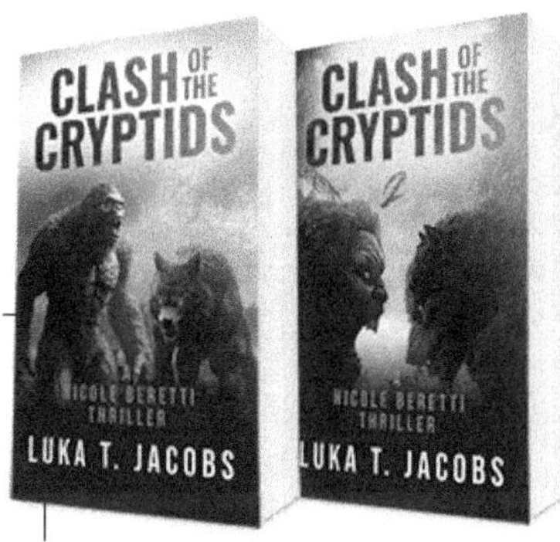

"Loved the first two books. I couldn't put either one down till the end. Ms. Jacobs knows exactly how to weave a story together, and make it seem absolutely real, A talent unfortunately not seen enough now days.

Clash of the Cryptids 1 and 2, imho, are sheer perfection. Going from moments of tension to fear, then absolute terror. The characters are wonderfully written, even giving the POV of the Dogman and the Squatch. Can't wait for book 3!"

JIM. T, VERIFIED AMAZON PURCHASE

Clash of the Cryptids Part 1 and 2 are available on Amazon and www.LukaTJacobs.com.